Laurie and James are a monogamous couple with an occasional lover in James's best friend, Al. It is a casual, friend-with-benefits situation which suits them all, especially given Al's promiscuous lifestyle.

When Al is assaulted, however, Laurie and James are forced to confront the fact that their feelings for Al might be stronger than mere liking. But would free-spirit Al ever want more than what they already have?

Copyright 2017 by P.A. Friday

Published by
NineStar Press
PO Box 91792
Albuquerque, New Mexico, 87199
www.ninestarpress.com

Warning: This book contains sexually explicit content which is only suitable for mature readers. Brief mentions of graphic violence and oral gang rape after the fact.

Print ISBN # 978-1-945952-44-9
Cover by Natasha Snow
Edited by B.J. Toth

LOVE PLUS ONE

Maths

P.A. Friday

DEDICATION

To Nikki, who loves these guys almost as much as I do.

ACKNOWLEDGEMENTS

So many thanks are due. First to Nikki, for reassuring me that this story was worthwhile, then Sasha for encouraging me to send it to NineStar Press, and lastly BJ, who has done a wonderful job editing, hand-holding, and getting rid of my ridiculous overuse of commas. And also to my own boys, James and Cameron, who may never read this novel but are so very loved.

PART 1: LAURIE

CHAPTER ONE

Laurie and James were monog-*Al*-mous. They'd decided to call it that, as it pretty much summed up the situation. Monogamous and committed and totally exclusive...with a minor exception for a certain young man called Alistair Hitchins, known generally as Al, with whom they both slept—always together.

Laurie gave a smile, remembering the first time James had brought the possibility up, almost eighteen months ago now.

He and Laurie had been sitting up in bed. Laurie lit a cigarette, keeping it away from James, whom he knew hated them. James had given the cigarette a baleful glance.

"If I gave you something you really want," he said slowly, "would you do the same for me and give up smoking?"

Laurie, languid after good sex and definitely not expecting what was coming next, blew out a little cloud of smoke and said, "Dunno. Probably. Why? What are you thinking of?"

James looked away, lips pursed as if thinking. "Oh," he said casually, "Al?"

Laurie, halfway through taking another drag on the cigarette, choked. "*What*?"

Al Hitchins. An arrant flirt and shamelessly and cheerfully promiscuous. Providing there was a mutual attraction and his prospective partners weren't cheating on someone and didn't expect a relationship from him, Al would happily sleep with just about anyone. He'd flirted with Laurie for years, and Laurie had certainly been attracted to Al—most people were—but Laurie had certainly never seen anything serious in it. After all, Laurie was with James, and James was Al's best friend, had been since childhood. Laurie knew well that there was no way on earth that Al would have done anything to jeopardise that relationship—such as hitting on James's boyfriend. It had been easy enough, therefore, to accept Al's flirtatious remarks as no more than habit. And it could easily have stayed that way; it would certainly never have occurred to Laurie to take it any further until James mentioned it. Laurie had protested—of course he had—that the exclusive relationship he had with James was all he wanted or needed, but somehow...well...somehow Al had happened.

And that had been that. If thinking about the three of them together had been hot, it had turned out the reality was hotter still, and none of them had put up any objection at all to continuing a sometime relationship as a threesome. (Okay, that wasn't quite true. Al had managed one: "Not a relationship, James," he had protested. "I don't do relationships. Regular sex with my two favourite blokes.") For the past year, therefore, the three of them had indeed been having sex on a regular basis. Oh, and Laurie had also given up smoking. He had another fixation now.

Al was coming round tonight, in fact, and James was cooking dinner. Al sometimes teased that the only reason he visited was because James's cooking was so good. Laurie's part in proceedings was to wash up, and Al's to bring wine since he worked in a wine shop when he wasn't making short films.

The doorbell went whilst James was still in the kitchen, and Laurie ambled to the front door to let Al in.

"Take your time, why don't you?" Al greeted him cheerfully. "It's bloody freezing out here."

"Sorry, your lordship." Laurie was amused but opened the door wider to let Al through.

It was indeed a braw late-February night, and Al was shivering as he entered. His jacket (black, like pretty much all of Al's clothes—though there were few people less Goth than Al was) was too thin for the time of year, but something like that would never occur to Al in advance.

"I hope Jamie's cooking something good," he said.

"Hello to you, too," James yelled back from the kitchen. "And as if my cooking isn't always awesome!"

Laurie rolled his eyes. It was going to be one of *those* nights—where the young men carped and teased each other non-stop. And then usually started in on Laurie...or at least, Al did. Laurie was ten years older than the other two and had known them since they were kids; Al apparently saw this as giving him due licence to act like a bratty younger brother when he chose. Which then gave Laurie licence to treat Al like...well, not precisely a younger brother, exactly... But where Laurie and James's relationship was very much one of equals, Laurie was not at all averse to telling Al precisely what he needed to be doing, and ensuring obedience in any way he chose. (This, too, had been rather a surprise to Laurie, who hadn't known he harboured such instincts. But it seemed Al was rather good at bringing to the foreground various kinks and desires that Laurie had never known he had. No one seemed to be complaining.)

Al sauntered into the kitchen with a couple of bottles of wine, Laurie following him, and put them on the table before walking up behind James, who was concentrating on a pan on the stove. Al slid his arms around James, resting them on his thighs. He was several inches shorter than James, though they had similar dark hair and regular features; as children, the two had been mistaken for brothers more often than not, with Al—to his great indignation at the time—always pinned as the younger sibling. The misapprehension had probably been made more likely by James's mother having a tendency to consider Al as her second son—Al's own parents, in contrast, had had little interest in him and moved abroad a month after he started university, discouraging him from visiting more than once a year. He hadn't seen them for quite some time now. Laurie wasn't sure whether he had deliberately broken the connection or whether neither side had quite cared enough to contact one another. He didn't quite like to ask—Al rarely spoke about his family, understandably enough.

"Hey, James. What's cooking?"

"Hey, little bro."

James turned around in Al's grasp and then leaned down to press his mouth firmly against Al's in a way that should have been frankly illegal if they had really been related. Laurie had long since got over the nagging feeling that he ought to be jealous, watching his boyfriend kiss someone else; watching James and Al together was always a pleasure.

"Mmm," said Al, kissing back with enthusiasm.

The kiss went on for some time, passion undimmed and hands beginning to wander...until the pan behind James hissed.

"Shit," said James, turning back hastily.

"Well, the starter was good," Al said, "but what's for main?"

"Pan fried—slightly pan burnt, now—salmon with lemon mustard greens and ciabatta," James said, rueful about the salmon.

Al peered over his shoulder. "Looks fine to me. A little bit of black never went amiss."

"Thanks," said James dryly. It was unknown whether Al could make anything more complicated than a pot noodle.

"It'll be fine," Laurie said. "White or red, Al?"

James tutted. "It's salmon. Should be white."

"So conventional," Al teased.

"You'll have red then?" Laurie asked, raising an eyebrow. Knowing the answer.

Al's lips quirked at one corner. "White, thanks."

"Stop annoying James, then," Laurie said severely.

"Yes, oh ancient one." Al reached to get the wine glasses. He was as comfortable in their kitchen as they were, which was how they all liked it. "What's for dessert, in that case?"

James turned around from his place by the stove to meet Al's gaze with laughing eyes. "You, I thought," he fired back.

"Yeah, if your old man can get it up," Al said dismissively, deliberately provocative.

Laurie glared. It was *definitely* going to be one of those evenings.

The meal was a success, nonetheless. James had not, in fact, burnt the salmon, which was melt-in-the-mouth good. There was silence for the first few minutes, as they sated the worst of their hunger; then the conversation kicked in. Mostly about their plans for the week—which of them had to be where, when, and with whom. The meal was nearly ended when James asked whom Al was dating this week. While Laurie and James were happily committed solely to each other in Al's absence, Al was happily uncommitted, with a string of one-time dates and longer-term fuck buddies. He had two rules and two rules only: as well as never sleeping with anyone who wanted anything more than no-strings sex, the only people he would fuck without protection were Laurie and James. Apart from that, anything went. It suited him well, and while Laurie would not have lived like that in a million years, he had a very soft spot for Al with his charming honesty about who and what he was and who and what he wanted.

"Seeing Gemma on Saturday," Al said between mouthfuls. He was usually the last to finish—always hungry was Al.

Gemma was a long-term...*whatever*...with Al. She was amazingly beautiful—"far too gorgeous for Al," James had said ruthlessly—and a backing singer with a popular band. She spent a lot of her time on tour, but whenever she was back in London, she and Al met up on a regular basis. Regular enough for Al to have introduced James and Laurie to her, in fact, which was a highly unusual occurrence. Like Al, she enjoyed the restfulness of having a sex partner who didn't expect anything of her, so that she could go away and see whom she liked and yet still come back and meet up with Al when it was convenient for them both. In many ways, they made a perfect couple—their perfection based on neither of them wanting to be a couple at all. Al occasionally appeared in the background of media photographs, but no one had picked up on him yet, for which he was grateful. He might want to be known for his film-making but his sexual liaisons, whether with Gemma or with anyone else, were private. Strangely for such a seemingly outgoing man, he was extremely reserved about himself. Laurie reckoned he knew Al as well as anyone bar James did, but there was still quite a lot that Al kept hidden. And James would never tell Al's secrets, nor would Laurie ask him to.

"She still sees you, why?" James asked immediately.

Al smiled slowly. "Because I'm that good in bed, obviously," he retorted. "You wouldn't understand."

"No, I wouldn't," James agreed. "You're not that good."

Al raised two specific fingers in his best friend's direction. "Good job you can cook, Jamie." His eyes drifted to Laurie. "Of course, that doesn't explain why I put up with the ancient crock you hang around with," he added.

Laurie knew Al was doing it on purpose. He knew it damn well. It was still working. With an effort, he kept his mouth shut and did not respond to Al's provocation.

James, however, had a different approach. "You want him that much, do you?" he asked, laying down his knife and fork and sitting back to look at Al appraisingly.

Laurie tried to bite back his surprise. He had known that Al was winding him up, but James's response had suggested that it was something other than mere mischief. That Al was trying to provoke him to...to what? Action? What sort of action?

Laurie could think of a good number of actions he could take to put Al in his place. For the first time, he was tempted to try them out in full.

"I have no idea what you mean," said Al, his voice slightly *too* innocent.

"Don't you?" asked Laurie, suddenly appraising.

"No." Al looked down, but there was a tiny smile curving his lips. "Old man, I have absolutely not a clue."

"Right," said Laurie grimly, standing up and walking over to Al, who appeared hopeful rather than alarmed. "If I'm so much bloody older than you, I'm quite old enough to dole out punishments to disrespectful boys who need a lesson in manners."

"Me?" asked Al, his tone optimistic.

"You," said Laurie, grabbing him firmly. If James was bigger than Al, Laurie was an inch or two taller still, easily able to cope with a not-unwilling captive. He dragged Al into the sitting room, James following after and sitting down on the sofa as if to watch a good film. Laurie glared at him before tugging Al's trousers and pants down. He had a good idea that James had been angling for this as much as Al had. "Come on, over my lap."

He manhandled Al to the sofa, settling himself down on it and pushing Al over his lap so that his head was resting on James's thigh. James, clearly amused, was watching the two of them—Al, so evidently willing; and Laurie, who, stern expression or not, was nonetheless now preparing to enjoy himself.

"What now?" asked Al, his voice muffled against James's leg.

"You, my lad, are going to get spanked thoroughly enough that even you will have a lesson to remember," Laurie said. There had been a few other occasions on which he had slapped Al's arse, just once or twice, and the expression on Al's face combined with the beautiful pink which had suffused his usually pale skin made Laurie suspect that neither of them were going to be too distressed by this particular punishment. "Unless you want to offer me a grovelling apology now, that is?"

Al made a rude noise. "As if. Anyway, you are an old git compared to James and me. Face it."

"*You* face your punishment," Laurie retorted, getting in a first stinging slap.

"Ouch," Al cried, not entirely voluntarily. The slap had been quite hard.

Then again, as Laurie could feel from the lump against his leg, so was Al quite hard. The smack did not seem to have affected that too negatively. He smacked him again, more gently, alternating the arse cheeks until they were both a dusky pink, and Al was murmuring something which might have been pain but very much might not have been. One of his hands had tangled in James's top, and the other was clenching and unclenching against James's thigh; and when Laurie glanced at James, James didn't look at all unhappy about the situation. Al's mouth was down flush with James's cock, and when he muttered, he was muttering hot words almost into the placket of James's trousers. Laurie could feel himself getting hard, too; he rubbed his hand across Al's heated, rosy arse, and Al wriggled pleasurably.

"Enough of that," Laurie scolded, getting back to business.

He was slowly working up the energy levels, and Al began to moan, humping Laurie's leg as Laurie spanked him. That was one of the things about Al: he had no inhibitions about showing how he was feeling sexually, rubbing up against Laurie with ever-increasing urgency as Laurie continued to rain half-punishing blows down on his arse and the insides of his thighs.

"Fuck, that's hot," James murmured, his eyes fixed on what Laurie was doing with Al. Laurie looked up and smiled at his boyfriend—his perfect, amazing boyfriend—wondering how many people had a lover quite like James.

"I don't think he realises the seriousness of his offence," Laurie said severely, once again stopping to run his hands over maltreated red skin.

"I do," Al mumbled from James's thighs. "God, please, Laur..."

"Please what?" asked Laurie. "And don't you think it's time you stopped being such a fucking prick-tease to James and sucked him properly? Look at you, drooling all over his trousers without giving him the satisfaction you know you can. Shame upon you, Al."

Al groaned, fumbling with the fastenings of James's trousers without further complaint. All three of them knew how much Al liked to have a cock in his mouth, but before he turned his attention to business, he said pleadingly, "And you'll fuck me, Laurie? Please?"

"Have you learned your lesson?" Laurie asked, the stern expression giving way to a grin where Al couldn't see it. Al could probably hear it in his voice, though. Laurie didn't really mind.

"Yes. God, I'll never call you names again...until next time I do," Al promised feverishly but with a beautiful level of accuracy. "I promise."

Laurie laughed and ran his hand very, very gently over the tender, hot arse of his sometime lover. "Wait there."

"Mm-hmm."

Al already had his mouth full, licking James with the wholehearted eagerness which he always gave to such a task. By the time Laurie came back with lube, Al was well away, rubbing himself off against the cushions of the sofa as his mouth worked up and down James's cock with little sighs of pleasure. Laurie stood by the sofa and watched for a moment before bending down to kiss his boyfriend hard on the lips. James clung to him for a few seconds, deepening the kiss before letting go.

"Well, then." Laurie slathered lube onto a finger and ran it round the rim of Al's hole teasingly before sliding it inside. It glided in easily, Al's body almost seeming to welcome it in; and it wasn't long before Laurie had added a second, scissoring them inside him.

Al pulled off James long enough to shift onto his knees and say, "Now, Laurie, please?" before returning to his appointed task.

Laurie was happy to oblige, pushing into Al and holding himself there gently. He didn't want to thrust too hard; the feeling of him against Al's punished arse would be uncomfortable for Al, and he had no intention of actually hurting the young man. So his thrusts were lazy and slow, and Al's mouth was deep down around James's cock, and it was magic sometimes—the three of them, at moments like this. Al rocked back against Laurie hintingly, and Laurie thrust a bit faster until they were all hot and sweaty and coming; Laurie had no idea in what order, only that five or ten minutes later they were all three lying sated in a complicated tangle of bodies on the sofa, and Laurie was feeling bloody marvellous.

There was silence for a while, and then Laurie met James's eyes, and in a moment or two, they had wriggled round a bit and Laurie's mouth was on James's, fingers tangling through his hair.

"Love you," he murmured in James's ear.

"Love you too."

There was a sigh and an audible rolling of eyes from Al. "Okay, guys, if we've got to that stage, I'm off. I'll leave you to your lovey shit."

"Okay," said James, with the callousness of a best friend, turning back to Laurie.

"You might want a shower first," Laurie added, flicking a glance at him.

Al gave a laugh. "I might at that. Don't worry about me. I'll see myself out." He waited until James and Laurie had returned to kissing and then added casually, "You don't mind if I just borrow a top, do you, James? Thanks."

Laurie suspected that James hadn't really processed this. He knew damn well that Al had intended that he shouldn't. James had a rooted objection to 'lending' Al clothes, complaining that they either didn't come back at all, or they came back with suspicious stains on them, meaning that James never quite wanted to wear them again. However, Laurie wasn't going to mention it. For a start, he and James were sharing rather a great moment, and for another thing, James and Al had been best friends for well over a decade, and there was no way in hell Laurie was going to walk into the middle of that can of worms. He gave himself up to snogging James, and neither of them noticed when Al actually left.

A couple of hours later, warm and loved up, Laurie leaned his head back on the arm of the sofa and gave a deep sigh of contentment.

"I like Al, but I do like it when it's just you and me," he said, stretching lazily.

"Me too." James ran a hand down Laurie's face. "God, I fancy you."

"You were kind of implying that," Laurie said, smiling. His gaze caught the clock. "Fuck, it's past midnight. I've got to go to sleep. I've got a lecture at nine tomorrow morning. Cinematography." Laurie was a film studies lecturer at the university. He loved his job, but he had the guilty knowledge that he had been intending to look over his lecture notes this evening, before he had got sidetracked by Al and James—and then by James. He swung his legs off the sofa regretfully. "And I'm going out with the department in the evening, so I'll be back late. What sort of day have you got?"

"Starting at twelve in the shop and then a couple of lessons with teenagers after school," James said. He taught guitar at a music school and worked in the associated shop at other times. "See you when I see you tomorrow, then."

"I won't wake you if you're asleep in the morning," Laurie promised.

James gave him a grin. "I will be."

James slept like the dead, given half a chance. Laurie needed to leave at eight in order to have time to get a coffee before lecturing, and James quite frankly thought that any hour before nine in the morning was the crack of dawn. He'd happily teach guitar 'til nine at night, but ask him to do anything before ten a.m. at your peril. Laurie gave him a kiss and headed for the bathroom.

"See you in bed."

CHAPTER TWO

Laurie hadn't expected the subject of Al Hitchins to raise its head the next day. His teaching went well enough, and he caught a bite to eat with a friend from the English Department, Gillie. He'd known her for more than fifteen years—since he was a student himself, in fact.

"Hi, Laurie," she greeted him, giving him a big hug. "How are you?"

"Fine." Laurie smiled at her. When he'd been a shy undergraduate, he'd known Gillie online as 'theflygirl'. After they'd realised she actually taught at the very same university he attended, she'd invited him round, and he'd become a regular guest at her and her husband, Terry's, house. Terry, who'd had multiple sclerosis all the time Laurie had known him, had died a couple of years previously; and Gillie had been devastated, even though both of them had known before their marriage that it would happen at some point. The form of MS that Terry had was known for its terminal nature, unfortunately. But they had enjoyed twenty-five years together first, after meeting at eighteen. "How's Roger doing?"

"Come on, let's get something to eat," Gillie said. "Roger's fine." Roger was Gillie's large ginger cat, an animal she'd got six months after Terry's death for companionship. They were inseparable when she was at home; Roger had only to see Gillie to jump on her, purring like a freight train—and weighing practically as much, in Laurie's opinion. He was an enormous animal. "He was sick the other day and frightened me into fits, but he seems absolutely fine now, and apart from that, all is well. How's James?"

And oh yes, that was the other thing. Because Gillie also happened to be James's mother. In fact, Laurie had first met James when James was an enthusiastic ten-year-old with a passion for Harry Potter, Doctor Who, and—considerably more unexpectedly (and, in general, extremely privately)—My Little Pony. Laurie had been in turns amused, annoyed, and then, very guiltily, attracted by Gillie's son as he grew up. It had taken Laurie a long time to forgive himself when he'd first realised that he'd started thinking of James in a sexual manner. James had been nineteen then, and open about his own feelings for Laurie, but Laurie had run a mile at the very suggestion.

Laurie and James had been together for two and a half years and living together for the last fifteen months of that, but Laurie still got a bit weirded out by the fact that he was dating his best friend's child.

"Not too bad at all. Snoring his head off when I left him this morning, in fact," Laurie said, stretching the truth a little bit as James didn't actually snore. "Still can't believe you are still talking to me, by the way."

"What, because you're sleeping with James?" Gillie had a mischievous look that was unnervingly similar to her son's sometimes. "I was more inclined to shake you hard when you were ignoring him, and he was pining over you, if you must know. Stubborn wretch that you were. I could see you were in love with him, but there was absolutely nothing I could say if you weren't going to admit to it. And James made me promise I wouldn't talk to you about him."

Laurie showed a sudden interest in the menu. He hadn't realised he'd been quite so transparent.

"I...um...think I'll have nachos," he said evasively.

Gillie, mercifully, changed the subject. "I considered that, but I can't resist their prawn gumbo," she said. "So. What have you been up to lately?"

"Al was round last night."

Gillie laughed. "My second son?" After Al's parents had moved away, his home in the holidays had been with Gillie and Terry. And he'd spent so much time there in his teens that he'd already had his own bedroom—though, as he liked to remind Laurie, he'd been thrown out to sleep on a mattress on James's bedroom floor when Laurie stayed the night. "Still can't get rid of him, then?"

"Apparently not." Laurie smiled. "I'll live."

"Yes. I gather his new film's doing quite well," Gillie said.

"Is it?" Laurie was faintly embarrassed that he didn't know. He knew the film itself, *Welding the Night Away*—and loved it—but hadn't the faintest idea whether it was a critical success or not. Call himself a film lecturer, and Gillie still knew more about the status of Al's film than he did. Mind you, he'd got a little distracted the night before. "That figures. Al's generally good at what he does. He's still known as one of the best students in recent years, you know." For Al had studied Film Studies at the university up until a few years previously.

"He is that."

The two of them gossiped about various subjects over their meal. Gillie was always good company, and it was lovely to see her without James being present. They had a different sort of relationship in his absence—Gillie could go back to being Laurie's best friend, not his mother-in-law equivalent. It was half past seven by the time they finished chatting, and Laurie had to head straight over to meet his workmates.

They were going to a pub often frequented by students, which wasn't always the best policy; but on the other hand, it sold the cheapest drinks locally, and they all liked the atmosphere there, so it tended to be the group's go-to place. There was a group of five of them, with little in common save their jobs; but they got on well, and Laurie always enjoyed the evenings out. His closest workmate was Polly, a woman about five years older than him, who specialised in horror films and in particular in special effects. Laurie especially enjoyed watching her walk into the opening lectures where the students were introduced to a number of different lecturers and told about their special interests. Everyone looking at Polly, with her blonde hair and perfect make-up, expected her to be specialising in romance; when it turned out that she was an expert in the most unpleasant moments in age-eighteen horror, there was often a slight gasp from the students, hastily suppressed. Greg and Simon did more practical, camera-based work, taking students out and teaching them the basics of film. Al, Laurie knew, had given a few talks to some of their classes in the past. Annabel, in her early sixties, taught about films from the 1920s to the '50s with a secondary interest in the making of films from books. Laurie had been slightly intimidated by her to begin with, as she always seemed to know everything, but her wry sense of humour and complete lack of superiority had won him over. When he'd studied for his PhD, she'd been his supervisor, and he knew that her help had been invaluable. What was more, she might be fifteen years older than the oldest of the rest of them, but a night out without Annabel wasn't a night out worth mentioning.

They talked and laughed, drinking and joking as the pub filled up with students. Although it was commonly known as a student pub, no one seemed surprised to see lecturers there, and it was a convivial atmosphere. At least, most of the time. Laurie had got up to get some more drinks in when he heard the comment. It was from a film student of his—David something—and he'd had no intention of eavesdropping on any other conversation, but David did have a particularly carrying voice.

"Yeah, well, a disgusting faggot prossie like Al Hitchins deserves to get a good fucking punching. He's got it coming to him."

Al's name as a local short film-maker—and, indeed, one who was beginning to get international attention, albeit in a minor fashion—meant that it wasn't surprising when Laurie's students had heard of him, especially if they'd attended any of Greg or Simon's classes. But this was different. Before he knew what he was doing, Laurie had turned back to David's table, put one hand on his wrist, and was speaking quietly in his ear.

"As your lecturer, I think I should warn you that homophobic insults, especially linked with threats of violence, could get you into a lot of trouble," he said, his fingers tightening a little on the young man's wrist. Laurie wasn't proud of it—in fact, he was rather embarrassed by the fact—but he couldn't help but be aware that he was considerably larger and stronger than most people he knew. He went out of his way to hide his strength most of the time, even if he couldn't hide his size, but this wasn't most of the time. "And on a personal level," he added, his voice quieter still, "I should advise you that, before you make any other comments about Al Hitchins, you decide how much you value the use of both your arms. I hope I make myself clear."

He did not wait for a reply but turned back to the bar. His heart was thumping rather uncomfortably; it was not his style to make threats—in fact, Laurie couldn't remember ever having done such a thing in his life—and he was still not sure what had come over him, but for once in his life, he had seen red. He was used to seeing himself as a relatively peaceful bloke; most people described him as, if anything, a little bit too laid back. He stammered an order for three beers and took them back to the group, who were staring at him.

"Sorry about that," he said, flushing.

"Don't be," Polly said briefly. "I heard what he said, too; if you hadn't said something, I would've done. It was bloody offensive."

The other three nodded. They all knew Al, both from his talks and his time at the university. Annabel had rated him then—rather to Laurie's surprise at the time—as one of the best students she'd ever taught. Polly didn't know him as well as the rest, but the tenor of the remark by David had been offensive enough that even had it been about a complete stranger, the point would still have stood. Laurie suspected that none of the others knew quite how well he knew Al—at least, he was certain they didn't know that he was sleeping with the younger man, since no one but Al and James knew that particular fact. But he was also fairly sure that they didn't realise that Laurie's boyfriend was Al's best friend. However, their support was welcome.

"Seemed a bit out of character for you," Greg explained, "but then I didn't know what the guy had said until Polly filled me in."

"That's David. David..." Laurie struggled to remember. "David Ironside. He's in one of my seminar groups," he explained, as if that made it better. Shit, that was going to be an interesting seminar later in the week. What had he been thinking?

He'd been thinking, Laurie reminded himself, that no one was going to say anything like that about Al without getting into a whole host of trouble. Except Laurie had put himself in more trouble than his student had. Had he really threatened a student in the middle of a crowded pub? Thank god, his fellow lecturers hadn't actually heard what he'd said; Polly might have caught David's words, but Laurie had made damn sure that his own voice in response was low. Not, in fact, because he'd been worried about what they might think, but because he had emphatically not wanted there to be more of a scene than there already had been. A few people, no doubt, had heard what David had said; but hearing Laurie's response to it would have given it more impetus than it already had. It was, no doubt, just a stupid drunken comment; no need to make it into something more by starting a major brawl.

God, he was stupid. Why had he said anything at all? Except, how could he let someone slag off Al like that and *not* respond? Al was James's best mate, yes—but he was more than that. He was James's and Laurie's lover, and Laurie's very dear friend, and no one—but no one—was going to say things like that and get away with it.

"I've got to say, I didn't know Al Hitchins was gay, though," Simon commented. He took a sudden conscious look at Laurie. "N-not that there's anything wrong with it, I mean," he stammered.

Laurie's anger was subdued beneath amusement at his workmate's embarrassment. It was odd the way some people still found the subject awkward. "I didn't think you meant there was."

"And he's not," Polly added unexpectedly. "Al, I mean."

Laurie looked across the table and raised his eyebrows, knowing precisely what was meant by that response. Now, *that* was unexpected. He hadn't thought Polly really knew Al. Though, if she did, it was perhaps unsurprising that she knew him quite so intimately. She might be forty or so, but she was extremely attractive; and Al was—well, appealing in his own way, as Laurie knew all too well. She gave him a small smile across the table, silently confirming his conclusion. He smiled back. There was a certain pleased look that tended to come into the faces of anyone who had slept with Al when they thought about the experience, which spoke well for the young man. It was rather endearing.

"Nor, to be fair, is he a prostitute," Laurie pointed out, leaving the subject of Polly and Al to one side.

"Indeed," Annabel agreed, "it is the principle of the making of the comments rather than their accuracy which was in need of correction."

"Sorry about that," Laurie said again, realising that beneath it all he was still simmering with anger. He took a long draught of beer.

"I don't think any of us are criticising you in the slightest," Annabel said in her precise voice, the bottle of wine she'd bought earlier in the evening close to empty. She glanced across at the table where David now sat, somewhat silently, with his friends, and raised her voice enough to make sure that he could hear. "Unacceptable behaviour should be challenged wherever it is met."

Laurie gave her a look of deep gratitude. He knew, even if she didn't, that her words might just have saved his job. Of course, Annabel didn't know that he'd threatened physical harm against a student. David, however, didn't know that she didn't know. Supported by his fellow workmates, Laurie was in a much better position—even if they'd be the first to criticise him if they knew the truth. Which they mustn't. No one must know the truth. That was fine, because Laurie was never, ever, repeating any of it—not what David had said, and definitely not how he'd responded.

They stayed for another couple of rounds. Annabel finished her bottle of wine and left. Simon took a look at his watch and said, apologetically, his wife would be expecting him.

"I'm on bottles tonight," he said, referring to his eight-month-old daughter, Mia, who had recently moved from boob to formula but was still, alas, incapable of staying asleep for an entire night.

Polly, Greg, and Laurie drank a little more—it was Friday, after all: no teaching the following day—but finally, they departed to their different homes. Laurie felt the shock of the cold air against his skin as he left the pub, realising as it flickered and tickled against him that he'd had slightly more beer than he'd bargained for. Never mind. It had been a good evening... It *would* have been a good evening, if it hadn't been for That Incident. But he would forget That Incident. Yes. That would be the right thing to do. If he didn't think about it again, it wouldn't have happened; and he could face David in the seminar next week with nary a look of embarrassment.

Denial. That was the way to go. Laurie nodded to himself like a wise old owl, and headed home. When he got there, he fumbled with the key in the front door a couple of times, trying to convince himself that it was the darkness and not the beer. Of course it was. He got in to find James sitting on the arm of the sofa, guitar on his lap, strumming. Laurie tried to work out whether it was something he knew or something new that James was working on. James was extremely shy about his music. He'd only write new pieces when Laurie was out of the house for some reason or other. He had featured on the score of Al's recent film, playing pieces he'd composed, but had insisted that his name was kept out of things, his initials representing him instead. Still, there was something about James playing his guitar which turned Laurie on. It always had, even when he'd been trying to deny his attraction to the younger man. Seeing him now, Laurie felt a familiar throbbing sensation start up in his groin.

"Hey, good evening?" James asked, looking up.

"Yeah. No, not really," Laurie said. "Bit of a...bit of a..." He stumbled to a halt, not sure how much to tell James of what had happened in the pub. Not really wanting to say what he'd heard about Al, and definitely not wanting to admit how he'd reacted. He changed the subject before the conversation could all accidentally spill out of his rather too-lubricated mouth. "Saw your mum for tea. Awesome woman, your mum. Great. Love Gillie. She's wonderful."

"You're pissed," said James, his tone resigned.

"Maybe a bit," Laurie admitted. "Still, I do. Love your mum, I mean."

"Yeah, I know. Look, shut up about my mother, okay?" James suggested. "How was the rest of the evening? And what was the 'bit of a' that there was?"

"Oh, erm..." Laurie came further in, leaned down, and kissed James hard. "God, that was good. Doing that again." He kissed him again and fought with the urge to tell James everything. "Yeah, nothing much. Just had a bit of an argument with a student. Homo...homophobic threats, and I told him he was an arse."

"You..."

"No, no, didn't do that," Laurie corrected himself hastily. "Said that as his lecturer I needed to advise him not to make comments like that. Sensible thing to say." Definitely glossing over the bit about Al and forgetting entirely the bit about threatening a student, having seen the expression on James's face just then. Not something to bring up. No. "God, you're hot," he said instead, pulling James into a hug.

"Mind my guitar," protested James, putting it down carefully.

"Sorry. Sorry. But you're hot. You're gorgeous; you are."

"Laurie, love, you're p—"

Laurie could see the word 'pissed' on the end of James's tongue again and hastily kissed him before he could get it out. "Shh. Wanna snog you. Wanna..." He had his hands all over James, touching him everywhere. James, half laughing, half protesting, was making a bit of an effort to push him off, but Laurie was persistent.

"I'm sure it's immoral to take advantage of you when you're this drunk," James said.

"Let me take advantage of you, then," Laurie said immediately, pushing his hands underneath James's clothes. "God. Probably too drunk to fuck you. Let me suck you off, James, please."

"Laurie..."

"Jamie," Laurie said, looking deep into James's eyes. "Please." He got to his knees in front of James, running his hands down James's trousers, fingers light-tipped on James's erection. James was hard for him, whatever he was saying. "Come on, let me."

James sighed, carding his hands through Laurie's hair and giving tacit permission for Laurie to undo his trousers and pull them down. Laurie tugged James's cock free.

"Love your cock. Love you, James," he said, pressing kisses to the tip and then the sides of it. "So beautiful."

His mouth was greedy on James's cock, desperate for him, wanting to taste every last millimetre of him. His hands pushed up under James's shirt, touching the taut, warm skin of his belly and chest. James hissed in a breath.

"Laurie," he said again.

"Mmm," said Laurie, his mouth busy on James's cock, his hands continuing to touch and tease, running back round until his fingers splayed on James's arse. He stroked lightly and then pulled James in tighter to his mouth, sucking and bobbing and taking him deep, deep into his throat.

James groaned and started thrusting despite himself. Laurie revelled in his boyfriend's loss of control, sliding fingers down James's legs and the insides of his thighs as his mouth worked long and hard on James's cock. James came in a burst down his throat, a long deep moan slipping from his mouth as he did so. Laurie swallowed as much as he could, the remainder dripping down the side of his face as he nuzzled into James's crotch.

"God, love you so much, James. Love you. Could just kneel here all night at your feet."

James's arms had gone around him, holding him against his legs. They were warm and it felt so, so good, and the moment seemed to stretch on forever. Finally, though, James sighed and leaned down to pull Laurie up.

"Come on. You ought to be in bed. You're going to feel awful in the morning." He yanked his trousers back up around himself and fastened them firmly.

"'ll still love you," Laurie mumbled, catching his arms around James even as they walked towards the bedroom.

"Love you too, you idiot." James was pushing him onto the bed, undressing him, bending down to take Laurie's shoes and socks off. "You can shower and brush your teeth in the morning. Now, just get to sleep."

Chapter Three

By Thursday, when Al came round again, Laurie could convince himself that the previous Friday night hadn't happened. Well, not the blow job—that had been spectacular. He would happily spend half his life on his knees sucking James's cock if he thought he could get away with it. But the earlier bit in the pub. Laurie firmly cancelled it all out—not just his reaction but what David had said in the first place. It was nothing, just a stupid comment. He'd overreacted. It was all totally not worth thinking about again. Especially with a bright-eyed and bushy-tailed Al on the doorstep, holding a couple of bottles of wine and coming in all guns blazing with his conversation about the latest film based on the Marvel comics.

Al, bless him, was a shameless geek and knew the original comics as well as the films. Laurie vividly remembered a younger Al rabbiting on endlessly about the different attributes of various Avengers and which he'd put in his fantasy football team. Laurie had groaned and rolled his eyes; Gillie had been more sympathetic (possibly because she was considerably more interested in football than Laurie was, and could comment wisely on the possibilities of putting Iron Man at left-back rather than as a striker; or possibly because, being thirty-something rather than in her early twenties, she'd had rather more patience than Laurie with Al's obsessions). James had cheerfully stated his blank ignorance on both subjects and instead suggested which Star Wars characters would best replace the musicians in Queen. (Han Solo, as Laurie recalled, had been Freddie Mercury; he himself had put in a vote for Obi-Wan Kenobi as Brian May. Hey, he had never claimed not to have geeky interests; it was merely that the Avengers weren't some of them. Gillie and he had met, after all, on a Lord of the Rings discussion board.)

"Another of your T-shirts on today, I see," he said to Al, referring to the fact that Al had a great number of fandom-related shirts with messages and comments across them.

"Of course." Al grinned. "I was out with Gemma on Saturday wearing my Star Wars one. You'd've approved. Well, actually, you probably wouldn't have done, but she did."

"What's this one say?" James asked, craning to look. "Ooh, I like that."

Laurie examined it. James would like it, of course; it was Harry Potter related, and his boyfriend had never lost his childhood fondness for the Potter books. *Even Pure-Bloods Marry Muggleborns. Get Over It,* the T-shirt read—a reference to the arguments over gay marriage as well as Harry Potter. He nodded appreciatively.

"Nice. Amazed it's not the Avengers, though."

Al gave Laurie a look from under long eyelashes. "I wore this one for Jamie's sake, of course," he purred. "Thought it might turn him on."

"You're impossible," said Laurie, at the same moment as James said, "I do not get turned on by T-shirts, thank you so much."

Al laughed. "Oh well, it was worth a try."

"He prefers you with it off," Laurie suggested, and James gave him a glare.

"Whose side do you think you're on?"

"I'm on the dinner-maker's," Al—shameless with his enormous appetite—said.

James frowned at him. Laurie knew that James worried that Al didn't eat properly when James wasn't there to keep an eye on him. Personally, he thought James was fussing too much—from what Laurie had seen of Al's body, it was in perfect shape. Slim, he certainly was; but he was by no means underweight. But James was not so easily convinced.

"It's pesto chicken pasta," he said briefly.

Al went over to him and gave him an extravagant, overdone hug. "Jamie, I am most certainly on your side. If you say you don't like the look of me without my shirt on, then you definitely do not."

"I didn't say that, either," James protested, giving Al a shove. "You two are both impossible; I don't know why Laurie's claiming it's just Al. And I'm going to finish the dinner. Someone open some wine, please. Mine's red."

"But it's chicken, James," Al protested, eyes wide and innocent. "Isn't chicken supposed to go with white?"

"Fuck off, Al," James said good-humouredly and pattered back into the kitchen to cook.

The meal was as good as all of James's cooking was. Laurie knew he was lucky to live with someone who not only cooked beautifully but loved to do it; and Al was always appreciative of good food. Or, possibly, *any* food. Laurie and James tended to comment that it was one of the few times they could get a word in edgeways as Al addressed himself to his meal as much as to conversation. For someone so slight, he could pack food away. Laurie was pretty sure, watching him, that James had nothing to worry about. After dinner, they went out to the sitting room, where Laurie picked up the paper and started gazing through the crossword, occasionally reading out clues for the others to offer answers. James began to quiz Al on the last week's dates.

"Gemma, we know about," he said, "but wasn't there a guy you were seeing as well? The one you met at the wine shop?"

"Leo." Al looked sad for a moment. "No spark. Plus, I think I was a bit...dunno, something, for him."

"Did he run off screaming?" asked James, grinning.

Al grinned back. "Pretty much," he admitted. "Nice bloke. Lovely bloke—hope he finds what he's looking for. Gentle sort of chap. Pleasant."

"Bit dull?" James suggested.

"Or I was a bit weird—you pays your money and you takes your choice," said Al cheerfully.

One of the things Laurie liked about Al was that he was always nice about his lovers—potential, actual, or apparently not (as in this case). Clearly, the evening had not gone at all to plan, but Al always shrugged it off with a casual, positive comment.

"Sorry it didn't work out," Laurie said, looking up from the paper for a second.

"It happens." Al's eyes danced suddenly. "Rarely, because I'm just that good. But it happens. Great night with Gemma on Saturday, though. She appreciates me." He glanced over at Laurie. "She was admiring your handiwork, too, by the way. Very thorough, I'm informed."

"What?" Laurie was confused for a second, and then cottoned on, blushing. The spanking. Apparently, the marks had still been visible by Saturday evening. "Um, how's that been?" he asked awkwardly.

"It's been bloody awful. Haven't been able to sit down for more than two minutes all week," Al said lightly, leaning on the back of the sofa.

"God, sorry," Laurie said guiltily. Now he thought about it, hadn't Al been standing up more than usual tonight? Was he still in pain? Laurie hadn't meant to smack Al that hard; not to really hurt him. Fuck, he really ought to get a grip on his own strength sometimes.

Al pursed his lips, his eyes mischievous. "Yeah, it's been terrible. Every time I sit down, I can feel it, and I start thinking about how fucking hot it was with you slapping my arse and me sucking Jamie's cock, and I get so hard I have to get up and lock myself in the loo for a wank. My arm's bloody knackered, too."

"You..." Laurie half stood up as James laughed. "You tosser. I felt awful for a second then."

"Poor baby," Al mocked. "Want me to make you feel better?"

Laurie subsided back into the chair and picked up the paper again, glaring at him over it. "No. I'm going to finish the crossword. Go and snog James."

Al flashed a look at him. "Is that an order?" he asked hopefully.

Laurie looked across at James, who quirked a smile at him and shrugged, clearly happy enough with the idea. "Yes," he said, returning his gaze to Al.

"Oh good," Al murmured quietly.

He rolled himself over the top of the sofa and down and across to James, reaching up to pull James's head towards his. James responded willingly, and Laurie had to admit to himself that the crossword paled in comparison with watching the two young men kiss. They were startlingly similar in some ways: James was broader as well as taller than Al, but their body shape, as well as their looks, were alike. And both of them were very, very attractive, Laurie thought appreciatively.

"You can do better than that," he said critically, however. "Why don't you lie down, get a bit more serious about it?"

Al made a happy noise in his throat, and James manoeuvred himself so that he was lying next to Al, who managed to continue kissing him through all of the repositioning, lying against the side of James's body. And Laurie could watch that all day. Though there was still more that could be added.

"Properly on top of James, Al. James likes to feel a bit of weight on top of him, don't you, Jamie?" James didn't look up, managing to settle more comfortably under Al at the same time as raising his middle finger in a specific gesture in Laurie's direction. Laurie grinned. "You know you like that better, Jamie," he said, his voice soft and suggestive. James gave a little moan but repeated the gesture, his other hand nonetheless now wrapping round Al's waist and pulling him down firmly against him.

"God, James," Al murmured appreciatively, wriggling closer still.

Laurie's trousers were suddenly very, very uncomfortable. Two hot young men making out on his sofa, all slim hips and muscular bodies and—Laurie was pretty sure—hard cocks. Al was nibbling James's neck now, and James had given up on making rude gesticulations at Laurie in favour of tangling both his arms and legs around his friend. Laurie stroked himself hard through his trousers and wondered how far James and Al were prepared to go.

"Okay, James?" he asked quietly.

"Mm-hmm." James took his mouth away from Al's body and looked at Laurie for a second. His cheeks were flushed a delicate pink, and the pupils of his eyes dilated. Laurie couldn't blame him for being aroused; it was steamy enough just watching. "You?"

"Definitely."

"Is no one going to ask me if I'm all right?" Al demanded.

Laurie flicked him a glance. "You were the one asking for orders," he pointed out. It might not have been precisely what Al had said, but the meaning had been clear enough.

"Fair point," admitted Al.

"Now, James," Laurie murmured. "Take off Al's shirt for me, will you please?"

He watched James's long, slender fingers slide under Al's T-shirt, pushing it up over Al's shoulders. Al wriggled obligingly out of it, and Laurie's gaze rested thoughtfully on Al's chest. Al was slim, but not scrawny; his muscles were defined, and his pale skin was very, very touchable. Clearly, James thought the same way. He was running his hands over Al in an extremely possessive way, to which Al was not objecting in the least.

"Flick his nipples," Laurie ordered. "See what that does to him."

He'd done something similar to Al in the past, and the results had been rewarding. James, who was looking at Al with a lazy smile on his face, moved to obey. Al hissed and jerked at the touch, jolting his hips against James's over and over again as James repeated the motion.

"Mmm, like that," Laurie said appreciatively.

"Yes," agreed Al, a little breathlessly.

"See, in a minute, Al," Laurie said conversationally, "I'm going to get you to take off James's trousers and pants so you can suck his cock. You'll want to make it so slick and wet, too, because then I'm going to watch you ride him." Al gave a little groan, and James looked across once more at Laurie, who smiled at him. "Love your cock, James. I've never watched you fuck someone. Bet it's gorgeous."

"Yes you have," protested Al, who had been fucked by James before in Laurie's presence, and who was keeping an almost admirable level of concentration on the conversation despite James continuing to play with his nipples.

Laurie laughed. "I've usually been busy at the time," he said, referring to the fact that they were usually all three having sex. "This time, I'm just going to watch you ride my boyfriend. Make it good for him, Al."

Al gave him a sideways glance. "I will."

"I know," Laurie assured him. "But first you need to suck him. Make him all wet for you. Do you want me to find lube, or will that be enough for you?"

"Enough." Al gave a wicked smile. "I want to feel it all."

"You don't mind, do you, James?" Laurie asked.

"Hmm?" James was busy with Al's body, still rubbing one finger over one of his nipples whilst he scraped the nails of his other hand gently down Al's back. Al continued to rock against James as he talked, his hips never ceasing to push and thrust his cock against James's. "Oh, be my guest."

"Stop getting yourself off then, Al, and pay James some attention," Laurie scolded.

Al sighed. "You're always telling me that," he complained, but his tone was not serious, and he willingly wriggled down James's body to kneel on the floor beside him and remove his jeans and pants. James shifted his hips to allow him to do so, and Laurie found himself gazing longingly at James's gorgeous long cock, which was full and hard. Clearly, Al felt the same way; he murmured, "Oh," quietly before lowering his head to lick his way over and around James's erection.

Laurie watched the back of Al's dark head bob and move as his hands slid over James's thighs and held him still for Al's ministrations. There was a level of concentration in Al's posture, and his half-naked state did not decrease Laurie's appreciation of the scene in front of him. James's eyes were somewhere between open and closed, and he had one hand in Al's hair, stroking it with a repetitive movement, and pushing the long locks out of Al's eyes when they threatened to obscure his vision. The noises Al made around James's cock were obscene and incredibly hot; Laurie unzipped his trousers to give his hand better purchase on his own cock; no one could watch this and not be turned on. James was breathing faster now, his other hand clenching on the sofa cushion.

"Christ, Al," he said hoarsely. "I want to fuck—"

"Not his mouth, James," Laurie said quickly. "I want to see you inside him."

"God, whatever," James said, his body shifting involuntarily underneath Al's mouth.

"Trousers off, Al," Laurie said, stroking himself over and over. "I want you to impale yourself on James's cock. You know you want to."

It was clear Al did want to. He was already removing his trousers before Laurie had finished speaking, his mouth still busy even as he did so. He lifted his lips from James's cock long enough to suck a couple of fingers into his mouth, circling them with saliva before thrusting them inside himself, opening himself up for James's possession. Laurie, unable to help himself, stood up from the chair he had been sitting in and went round to perch on the arm of another chair, near to the sofa. James's head was close to him, his body stretching out, away from Laurie. Al knelt above James, dampening James's cock a little more with spit-slicked fingers before beginning to sink down onto it. Al was totally naked now; James half dressed. Laurie was fully dressed still, though he had pulled his cock free of his jeans to take it more firmly in hand. It gave a strange sense of the power dynamics, even as Al appeared in some ways the most in control, on top of James, in charge of the speed and depth of the fucking.

James reached out and stroked Al's cock with teasingly gentle fingers. In response, Al hissed and lowered himself further, harder, until he was all the way down.

"Don't fucking tease, James," Al said.

"Why not? 'S fun."

James had his most mischievous smile on, the one Laurie particularly loved. He continued to touch Al with light, soft gestures. Al made a little grumbling noise in his throat and started to move on top of James, the tempo fast and hard—thoroughly in contrast with James's motions.

Laurie's hand worked faster on his own cock; watching the two young men fight for dominance in this way was making his balls ache with need. Finally, Al began to get his way, and James's grip tightened on him, as if he could hardly help himself. Al was murmuring broken words under his breath as he fucked himself over and over on James's cock. He had sweat on his forehead and neck, slipping down his chest and making him glisten—hot in more ways than one. Under him, James was breathing harshly, hand and hips jerking in tandem. Laurie looked down at the desperate, needy expression on James's face, and it was almost all he needed to come.

Almost. The final straw was Al's sudden, bursting orgasm, milked out of him by James's musician fingers as if Al's cock were a very different sort of instrument. Laurie gasped and came, his come spattering Al's face and chest. The glazed, blissful look on Al's face was glorious; the way his mouth opened instinctively to taste as much of Laurie's come as he could, even as he rode the last stages of his own orgasm. It was enough. James jerked his hips once more and groaned as he spilled himself inside Al.

Deep harsh breathing. Deep harsh breathing and the smell of sex in the air.

"I knew that would be worth watching," Laurie murmured at last.

Al rolled onto his side, James's softening cock sliding out of him, and wiped his face, sucking a come-slicked finger into his mouth. "Call that watching?" he asked, grinning. "I call that joining in."

Laurie laughed. "You shouldn't look so hot fucking my boyfriend then, should you?"

Al leaned down and kissed James hard on the mouth. "Still hungry?" James murmured, his eyes closed. "Even now?"

"For you, Jamie," Al teased lightly.

Laurie knelt at the side of the sofa and kissed James in turn, soft and long and tender. "Everyone wants you, James," he said. "You're just that good."

James smiled, opening his eyes to look at Laurie. "Well, of course," he said. Then, more seriously, "Fuck, I'm done for now, though. You didn't want anything else useful out of me this evening, did you?"

"Intelligent conversation?" Al suggested mockingly. "Party games? A light meal with waiter service? A shower?"

"You can talk about showers!" Laurie riposted to that last. His gaze ran approvingly over Al, covered as he was in sweat and three lots of come.

"Why yes, I can." Al grinned. "I'd take James into the shower with me, but I don't think he could survive it."

"Plus he's my boyfriend," Laurie reminded him. The three of them didn't have rules, precisely, but it was understood that Al had sex with neither Laurie nor James without the other present.

"That too." Al stretched unselfconsciously and rolled off James, picking up his clothes. "Well, a solitary shower it is. You can send Jamie in afterwards if he wakes up."

"James can send himself," Laurie retorted casually. "He's not a brat who needs ordering about."

"No?" Al cast an amused look at Laurie, still kneeling by the sofa, and James, flat out on it. "If you say so." He made for the bathroom and left the other two together.

"You didn't mind?" Laurie asked James again when Al had gone.

James yawned widely and stretched, reaching an arm up and tugging Laurie down to him. "I think I can safely say I didn't mind," he reassured his boyfriend. "You did check."

"I know, but..."

"Shh," said James, effectually silencing Laurie with a kiss. "I didn't mind."

By the time Al was out of the shower, James had perked up enough to get into it himself and reappear damp but clean. Laurie cleaned up and then poured some more of the wine Al had brought, and they talked about Al's recent film release. *Welding the Night Away* was a thought-provoking story about a young woman named Helen, who struggled with severe anxiety, which made her literally shake with nerves. Unable to sleep for more than a few hours at a time, she spent the rest of her night-times in her garage, welding together amazing artworks that never saw the light of day but which, for a few, peaceful hours, stopped her limbs from trembling and allowed her to get the little rest she could. It was breathtakingly shot, and Fliss, the woman playing Helen, had brought Laurie to the verge of tears with her performance. But the storyline and the direction were Al's alone; and as a film academic, Laurie genuinely thought it was one of the best short films he'd seen in a long, long time.

It was interesting, too, listening to Al talk about his films. The passion that he showed so openly and without reserve in sex was clear in this other sphere, too; although he would always be the fun, teasing Al that Laurie and James knew and loved, it did not mean he was incapable of taking anything seriously. He brought warm enthusiasm and love to his film-making, which made him (as Laurie had heard from those who worked with him) an inspiration to work with; he was genuinely passionate about his work and was respectful to the art and science of what he did. Laurie had known Al since he was a child, and there was still something childlike about the awe and wonder Al brought to the world—his loving interest in everything he put his mind to. James always seemed the more thoughtful of the two, and in many ways he was, but one underestimated Al's seriousness at one's peril. The first bottle of wine was finished and the second broached, and the three talked on through the night until once more Laurie knew that he would be underslept (though not underprepared—he'd worked the night before in preparation) before lecturing the next morning.

Finally, Al yawned. "Well. Got to be off," he said, standing up.

"Someday, we'll get you to spend the night," James said, blinking tiredly at him.

Al grinned. "Well, some day. Someday always comes. For now, I'm going to let Laurie tip himself into bed—he looks knackered. You should've reminded me that he does morning stuff, Jamie. I'm never going to remember that sort of thing."

James looked a bit guilty. "I never do, either."

Laurie laughed, standing up to give Al a hug before he left. "I'm probably old enough to go to bed by myself if I need to," he pointed out mildly.

"Mm, probably." Al deliberately injected a note of disbelief into his voice as he hugged Laurie in return. "Won't see you next Thursday, incidentally—I've got a date. Gemma can't do Saturday, and I promised we'd meet up before she's off on tour again. I'll be in touch."

"Mind you are." James waved an idle hand at him, and Al rolled his eyes but bent down to hug his best friend anyway, giving him a swift kiss.

"You can't get rid of me," he assured them both and sauntered to the door.

CHAPTER FOUR

It was a quiet week without the promise of Al coming round the following Thursday. Not unpleasant—James and Laurie went out together on the Tuesday, flirting shamelessly in public before coming home and tumbling into bed together, making sure that Laurie was thus as tired on Wednesday as he so often was on Friday mornings. On Wednesday night, James was teaching until late, and Laurie caught up on a lot of his marking—the endless burden of a lecturer.

It was surprising the way the people who could say the most interesting things in seminars were reduced to platitudes when required to express themselves in writing, whilst others who barely said a word were suddenly waxing lyrical on the history of Gothic horror. Laurie loved the different insights he got into his students through the different measures of communication; he might, as a matter of course, complain about his work, but he loved it nonetheless. Introducing new students to aspects of film they had never considered was a constant pleasure.

It was one thing which all three of them had in common—their dedication to their different jobs. For none of them, Laurie realised, was work merely a way to make money. At least, perhaps Al's wine shop work was such, and Laurie knew that James wasn't a natural salesman, despite working in the music shop—but their instinctive creativity made a bond between them which was never spoken of but was nonetheless strongly there.

Of course, it was very different from Al than it was between James and Laurie. Al...well, Laurie had heard the term 'free spirit' used on many an occasion, both as praise and in a pejorative sense...but Al epitomised the central idea of being a free spirit. Neither James nor Laurie could be called conventional in the strictest sense—their relationship with Al made that impossible, for a start—but compared to Al, they were extremely orthodox in outlook and behaviour.

Laurie sometimes thought they were a normal couple who had somehow been ambushed by Al into something different, but that wasn't fair. It had been James who had first suggested they sleep together and Laurie who had agreed without much argument. It was merely that Al was the sort of person who took one's normal ideas and bent them without even trying to do so. He would never have considered looking at either James or Laurie if they hadn't both been willing to have him, but when they had demonstrated their interest, Al was not the sort of person to turn them down.

At least, Laurie corrected himself, Al would have turned them down—in the gentlest, kindest way possible—if he hadn't been interested. But he had been; and they had been; and, with Al, to think was to do. Laurie could have been happy, ecstatically so, just with James. But he couldn't regret Al's entrance into their life together, no matter how unexpected. No matter how unconventional. It worked. It just worked. And that was all about it.

However, when the doorbell rang unexpectedly on Friday evening, Laurie wasn't expecting anything out of the ordinary. Instead, he was just mildly annoyed. It was 10:00 p.m.—well past the time when anyone should be calling on other people without warning, even on a Friday. And what was more, he was in the middle of the washing up after another of James's great meals.

"Oh, bloody hell," he grumbled. "James, I'm washing up. Could you—"

"Already on to it," James called back, making for the door. Curious as to who could be there, Laurie was half listening as he scrubbed the baking tray. But he would have heard James, even if he had been thinking about something else entirely. "Shit, Al!"

There was a note in James's voice that Laurie had never heard there before. Dropping the tray and giving his hands a cursory dry on his trousers, he sprinted for the door. He pulled up the second he saw Al, standing there in the semi-darkness of the landing. Al's top was torn, and his trousers had a ragged rip in them. He was wearing no coat; his hair was messed even more than usual; there was a livid red mark across the side of his face. But somehow, it wasn't about the clothes, but about the way Al looked. Eyes wide and dilated. Shaking, whether with cold or something else, Laurie couldn't tell.

Broken.

Terrified.

"I didn't know where else to come," Al said softly, his expression haunted. "Shit."

James's arms went round him, and Al suddenly had his forehead against James's shoulder and was sobbing hard. Laurie had known Al since he was a feisty ten-year-old, and he'd never seen him cry like this. Before he could think twice about it, he had his arms round Al too, holding him close in against James, Laurie's own solid body behind him.

"Come and sit down," he urged, half dragging the group of them towards the sofa.

"Sorry. God, so sorry." The words were tumbling out of Al's mouth as he cried. Laurie could feel the sobs shaking through his body. He was half frozen with cold, and damp too, and grimy. He looked—and smelled—as if he'd been rolling in the streets.

"Shut up," said James, with the brusque gentleness only the closest friend could manage in the circumstances. The sofa was beneath them, and he sank onto it, pulling Al with him. Laurie came too, kneeling beside the pair of them, one hand still protectively on Al's back.

"You don't have to talk about it," Laurie said carefully. "Not 'til you're ready."

"Laur..."

James gave him a pleading look, and Laurie nodded, getting up and going to the kitchen. He wasn't sure whether James wanted him to get Al a drink—his first instinct—or to talk to Al privately, away from Laurie. Close as the three of them were, Al and James's friendship was much longer standing. They were childhood best friends and trusted each other with everything. He poured a glass of water and a tumbler of whiskey, not sure which to offer, and hesitated in the doorway of the kitchen until he caught James's eye, and James jerked his head to motion him over.

"Told you. There were about five of them, and they just went for me," Al was saying, his head resting on James's arm.

Laurie made a policy decision and handed him the whiskey. Al took a gulp gratefully, and Laurie leaned on the top of the sofa, putting the water down on the table.

"But why?" James asked, his tone angry yet bewildered. Al scrubbed his face again with a hand and took another sip of the whiskey. "Not too much," James said, sounding like an anxious parent for a second.

"Fuck. I don't know. Because I'm queer? Because I'm openly promiscuous? Because I'm me?" Al hunched over. "I must've done something."

"No." Laurie could hear the furious shake in his voice but didn't know how to get rid of it. "No, you didn't." He grabbed Al's shoulders, forcing him up to look at him. "You did nothing wrong, Al. Don't you dare ever say otherwise." He saw James looking at him anxiously and made a determined effort to gentle his expression, his tone. "This is not your fault, Al," he said.

There were so many emotions running through Laurie. Fury, mostly. Sheer, hot, almost uncontrollable anger that anyone could hurt Al like this. Sadness, too, for the shaking, damaged mess which was his usually happy lover—a friendly, kind young man with no cruelty in his personality at all, yet people had felt able to do *this* to him. A wish that Laurie could do something, wave some bloody magic wand or something, and stop Al hurting. Make it right again.

And guilt. A sudden memory of what David Ironside, his student, had said a couple of weeks ago; how Laurie hadn't told James, hadn't given Al any chance to know what some people—some stupid, bastard, should-be-dead-right-now people—had been saying about him. Hadn't given him a warning. And now this. Which Laurie might, just might, have been able to stop, if he hadn't been so embarrassed. Not just embarrassed because of what had been said about Al, though that was bad enough, but at the awful, unprofessional response he'd had. If David had reported him for making personal threats, Laurie's job could have been in jeopardy. That wasn't the main reason Laurie hadn't mentioned anything to James, but it had been in there. Laurie had been worrying about his stupid bloody job, and now Al was here in tears, after several guys had... It still wasn't entirely clear what precisely they had done to him, but it was evident enough that it had not been friendly.

"We need to call the police," Laurie said abruptly, pushing himself upright from the back of the sofa as if he was about to go right over to the phone that second.

Al reached out and grabbed his arm. "No. God, please, don't." His eyes were filling with tears again, and Laurie could see the humiliation in Al's face as he rubbed them away. "Shit. You can't. Laurie, please."

Laurie sank down onto the sofa next to Al. "You can't just—"

"I can't tell anyone," Al said in a tortured whisper.

"James?" Laurie looked at his boyfriend.

"It's got to be Al's call," James said, his voice low. His arm was still slung around Al's shoulders; he didn't look as if he was ever going to let go, and Laurie was glad of it. Al needed that right now. Needed the grounding of knowing someone was there, right there, and wasn't leaving him for anything. "I wish he would, but..."

"Al," said Laurie, hating himself for what he was about to say. "Did they rape you?"

Al took a deep, shaking breath. "No...no, not—anally." He gave a weak smile, tried to look up and meet Laurie's eyes, but couldn't do it, his gaze falling back to his lap. "Just—just my mouth."

"Fuck, Al," hissed James, his grip tightening so much that it must have hurt Al, especially with the young man's bruises. But Al didn't object. He softened into James's touch, collapsing down against him, still shaking.

"It's okay," Laurie said, stroking Al with soft, repetitive gestures, though it wasn't, and it never would be. "It's okay. We're here."

"Yeah." Al swallowed another sob. "Thanks."

There was silence. The three of them sat there, helplessly. Laurie was still fighting the rage, the desire to go out and do physical harm to anyone who had hurt Al. James, when Laurie looked at his boyfriend, appeared torn apart. Al was his closest friend—much, much closer than most—and James would have given his life to make it better, but he couldn't. As to Al himself... It was now Laurie who blinked away tears.

"Am I so awful?" Al mumbled into James's stomach, where his head was pressed tightly against his friend.

"You're bloody brilliant," James said, his voice low. Then, clearly forcing himself, by stupendous effort, to a more normal tone, "And don't ever quote me on that. I'll deny it."

Al gave a sniff which was half a laugh, and Laurie looked at James with love in his eyes. James was dying inside, but Al didn't need that—he needed James's humour, the long years of banter which had covered so much emotion and love, so that was what James was trying to provide.

"I let you in the house, and I'm extremely fussy about my friends," Laurie added, doing his best to follow James's lead.

"Oh, I don't know," Al said, his voice still muffled by James's body, "you let James live here."

James was right, Laurie thought. Al was bloody brilliant to come back with that at a moment like this.

"There have to be exceptions," he said lightly.

"Are you up to more questions?" James asked, stroking the back of Al's head.

"Yeah." Al wriggled to sit up. "Sorry. God, I'm so sorry about this. Sorry."

"Will you stop bloody apologising?" James said, the words far harsher than the tone.

"You've nothing to apologise for," Laurie added.

"Yeah, I'm sure you get blokes turning up on your doorstep in the middle of the night demanding whiskey and sympathy every Friday," Al said.

"You're our best friend. You'd have something to apologise for if you didn't turn up on our doorstep when you needed someone," Laurie said. He put his hand carefully on Al's face where the red mark was turning slowly into a dark bruise. "We're quite fond of you for some reason."

"Still?" Al's smile was a bit wobbly.

"Shut up," James said again, giving him the smallest push. "And start talking. What the fuck happened?"

"What the fuck do you think?" Al snapped back. "Sorry," he said again. "Not on top form tonight. God, Jamie, I don't know. I was out celebrating, just a couple of drinks—*Welding the Night Away* just got nominated for a short film award and—"

"That's brilliant!" Laurie interrupted. "Sorry," he added, remembering the situation.

Al gave a more genuine smile. "No, it is. It really is. I'm so glad for the crew—they worked bloody hard on that. It meant a lot." He took a deep breath. "Anyway, when I came out, around nine, there were...well, a few guys. I was just heading on through, but one grabbed me and...shit, this still feels weird talking about it... He had a knife, and so we were down Norton's Street—you know, the dark one with the weird trees—before I really knew what was going on. So..." He shut his eyes for a second, and a shiver ran through him.

Laurie could see from his face that he was back there in the dark alley, with a group of men with a fucking knife, on his own. Laurie swallowed a lump from his own throat. "Yeah. They...uh...didn't seem keen on me, to be honest. Hit me about a bit, said a few things, then got me on my knees and..." Al stopped again, eyes wide open and looking at nothing. He put his hands hard against his face.

"Sorry. Wasn't very brave, I'm afraid. When someone's got a knife to your throat, you tend to pretty much do what they tell you to. I'd love to say I made a decent fight of it, but I did fuck all." He turned back to

James, his hand clutching James's arm. "Jamie, I fucked up," he said quietly. "I didn't mean to, but—"

"You didn't." James had pulled him very, very close, still showing no signs of letting go. Laurie knew how he felt. He wanted to do precisely the same thing. "You're here. God, Al, you did what you needed to do, what you should do. Christ." He was biting his lip as he met Laurie's eyes over Al's shoulder. Laurie could see that James was thinking the same thing as he was—of Al, alone with a knife at his throat. They should have been there. They should have been there to look after him. Their Al. Their Al, with a group of bastards forcing him to...

"Do you know who any of them were?" Laurie asked. He wanted to know. He wanted to kill them.

Al shook his head. "No idea. How could a group of strangers hate me so much, Laurie?" It was a plea from the heart.

"You were just there. Wrong place, wrong time," Laurie said gruffly.

"No," Al said quietly. He looked stricken. "That's the thing. Personal." He swallowed hard. "'That's him. Hitchins.' Then the knife. People hate me enough for...for *that,* and I don't even know why."

"What else did they say?"

Laurie saw that James was trembling now, even as he held Al. Laurie himself took a gulp of Al's whiskey to steady himself. Al curled himself up, as if trying to make himself as small as possible, perhaps disappear altogether.

"I—I can't..."

Laurie stroked his head. "It's just us. You can. You're safe."

"Faggot. Pervert. Whore." Al took a deep breath. "The usual sort of thing." Ever since he'd come out as bisexual at age seventeen, Al had been fielding insults to some degree. He'd let things wash over him with admirable aplomb. "Over and over, though. It feels a bit different when people are punching you and... Fuck. People hate me that much. I've always thought—just names—but—" He stopped.

"They're fucking idiots," said James fiercely.

"They don't know you. They don't know anything about you," Laurie added.

Al made a little noise. "Enough, apparently." He groaned as he uncurled himself, the bruises apparently beginning to seize up. "Fuck, sorry."

"Stop saying sorry," James said irritably.

"Such a bloody coward," Al muttered. "God, who the fuck gets attacked at nine o'clock? I thought... I was so fucking scared."

"You'd be the fucking idiot if you hadn't been," Laurie said bluntly. "Al, someone had a knife to your throat, for god's sake. Of course you were scared."

"Yeah. I don't know. Handled it like shit. So bloody humiliated. Maybe they were right about me."

"Fuck off," James said, loudly and angrily, grabbing Al's shoulder so hard that his best friend winced. "Don't you dare say that, ever."

Laurie placed his hand over James's, encouraging him to loosen his grip a bit. "Not precisely how I'd have put it, but James is right. You've done nothing wrong, Al. Nothing."

"Yeah." Al rubbed a few more tears from his eyes. "Anyway, that's pretty much all of it. God, I need a piss."

"You okay to sort that out?" Laurie asked, trying not to sound as overprotective as he felt.

"I expect I can manage a piss by myself." Al went to get to his feet, winced, and stumbled. "Shit, maybe not."

"Here." Laurie steadied him.

"Sorry."

"Stop saying that," James said automatically.

"Bruised?" Laurie asked.

Al nodded. "I guess."

"I'll run you a bath in a minute. 'Til then..." Laurie picked Al up with the carefulness one might reserve for fragile heirlooms, carrying him carefully to the bathroom. "Here. See what you can do about relieving yourself, and then we'll sort you out."

"Thanks. This is embarrassing," Al added, his voice slightly grim.

"You know what James would say," Laurie retorted, not quite able himself to tell Al to shut up.

Al pushed the door to, and there was the sound of urination and then of a tap running. When it finished, Laurie pushed in again, James behind him. James helped Al undress as Laurie ran the bath. Laurie could hear hissed breaths of pain from Al and a run of muttered expletives coming from his boyfriend so had some idea what to expect when he turned round to Al.

"Geez." The word came out before Laurie could stop it.

Al had a rueful look on his face. "Bad as that?" He tentatively stretched his arms out, trying not to wince as he did so.

Laurie couldn't reply. Al's brief "they hit me about a bit" hadn't got close to the whole story. Almost half of his body was marked in some way: bruises mostly, but with the odd scratch here and there, including a long, bloody knife cut down one leg, and something on his shoulder where Laurie thought he could see the indentation of separate teeth. Al's legs had suffered as much as his torso; Laurie suspected he'd been kicked about as well as punched from the shapes and positioning of some of the bruises. He felt somewhat sick.

"The hot water will help," he said practically, however, helping Al in. It was difficult to know where to touch him that he wouldn't rub up against a bruise, but Al seemed grateful nonetheless.

"Don't go away," Al said quickly, as if he was getting the words out before he could stop himself. "Sorry. Such a wuss."

"No, you're bloody not," insisted James.

"Don't suppose there's any of that whiskey left?" Al asked, making a determined attempt for light-heartedness.

"I'll get it." Laurie got up and went out to the other room. After looking thoughtfully at the glass, he went to the kitchen and poured another two for himself and James and then took all three back to the bathroom with him. As he approached, he could hear James talking.

"You're a bloody idiot," he was saying, but his tone was loving. "But thank god you had the sense to come here. And if you apologise again, I'll wash your hair and put soap in your eyes."

Laurie couldn't help grinning at this childish threat, wondering to himself whether the young men were old enough to be given whiskey to drink. But entering the bathroom, his mood sobered again at the sight of Al. Something Laurie hadn't noticed on the first glance was another cut on Al's throat; as he gave him the whiskey, he knelt down beside the bath and gently pushed Al's head back. The cut wasn't all that deep, but it was raw and unpleasant. The warm bath water had peeled back any scabbing which might have started, and it was oozing blood.

Al pushed away Laurie's hand. "Yeah, I think they were trying to tell me they were serious," he said briefly.

Laurie bit his lips together, hard, to prevent himself saying anything he would regret. Al needed to call the police. But James was correct; only Al had the right to decide whether to do that. Nonetheless, as he handed Al his whiskey in silence, he turned to collect up Al's clothes. Probably there would be no traces of DNA on them; but if any of the blokes had come, there was the possibility that some of their semen had left traces on Al's top. If so, Laurie was making damn sure there was a record of it. The clothes stank, but of a multitude of things—smoke, urine, and booze being the most obvious. The streets had no doubt been filthy.

"Thought we could do with a drink too," he said to James, handing him one of the other whiskeys.

"Not wrong there," James agreed. He looked at Al. "I'll find you some pyjamas or something."

There was a slightly panicked look on Al's face. "I'm not going to bed," he said hastily. "I'll be fine. I'll watch TV or something. Just... I can't..."

"Just, you can," James corrected. "If I have to put you in them myself, Alistair," he threatened, using Al's much-hated full name, "I'll do so. It won't be the first time."

There was a slight flush on Al's face when James said this, and Laurie took a moment to wonder about the first time that James had been obliged to insert Al into pyjamas against his will. However, this was probably not the moment to ask about it. Instead, Laurie said:

"Look, we'll get you all dry and in PJs, and then we'll all go to bed. Don't have to sleep. We can just be there together, okay?" He smiled. "It's a big enough bed, and James has been trying to persuade you to stay the night for ages. Give the poor bloke a chance." Al's gaze flickered between the boyfriends. He took another sip of his whiskey, and Laurie grinned. "You can bring that if you want, too," he said. "Alcohol isn't forbidden in the bedroom, you know."

Al gave a little sigh. "Sorry," he said, for the umpteenth time. "And thanks." He gave an embarrassed wince. "I may have to take you up on the help into pyjamas, James, much as it pains me to say it," he admitted. "Don't suppose you have painkillers, do you?"

"Apart from whiskey?"

Al gave a lopsided smile. "Yeah. Apart from that."

Between them, James and Laurie got Al dry, into pyjamas (somewhat too big for him; James teased him about looking like a kid in his older brother's clothes), and dosed with paracetamol, and then Laurie carried him through to the bedroom.

They didn't talk—not much. They lay there, Laurie on one side of Al, and James on the other, holding him. From time to time, they'd chat a bit, mostly about nothing in particular: about the size of the bed (easily large enough for three) or the fact that Laurie hadn't finished the washing up. Everyday things. Every so often, one of them would doze off for a bit, and the other two would exchange amused glances. Still, it was perhaps four in the morning before they finally went properly to sleep.

CHAPTER FIVE

Laurie woke up hard, about seven o'clock on Saturday. Half asleep, and with a warm, naked thigh pushing against his erection, he rutted against it dozily before he had time to think. His mind was murmuring something at him... James, yes, James didn't like being woken up in the morning, so this was probably not a great idea, even though this leg wasn't exactly like James's, more...

Shit. Laurie was suddenly properly awake, memories fizzing through him like electricity. More like Al, that body next to him. Al, who'd been raped by a group of men last night and needed like a hole in the head some tosser rubbing one off on him when he was supposed to be feeling safe somewhere. He opened his eyes and saw that Al, who had clearly climbed out of his pyjamas at some point in the night, was awake, lying on his back with his arms behind his head, staring up at the ceiling.

"Al. Shit, sorry," he apologised hastily.

Al turned his head to look at him and gave a quick smile. "Don't be. It was nice." He rolled over and kissed Laurie long and deeply on the mouth, his body curving into Laurie's. "Hot," he murmured, trailing kisses lower down Laurie's body, heading towards...

"Al. Don't."

It was a struggle to tell him to stop because Al was bloody good at this. But Laurie felt a horrible sense of guilt. Al wasn't in his bed for sex, not on this occasion. Laurie grabbed his wrists and went to pull him up, but Al looked up at him pleadingly.

"Let me. Please," he said. He took a shaky breath. "Can't sleep, can't stop thinking. I can still *taste* them in my mouth, Laurie. I need this. Please. Take the taste away."

"Fuck." Laurie let go of Al's wrists and rubbed a hand over Al's hair instead. "Whatever you want, Al. Whatever you need."

"Thank you." Al's voice was soft.

And that made Laurie feel like shit, if nothing else did—having Al thanking him for letting him blow Laurie. Except Al was so damn talented it was difficult to keep hold of any bad emotion. The feel of his warm, wet mouth laving down the underside of his cock, swirling Laurie's balls in his mouth was almost too much. Al swiped his tongue up and down and back until Laurie was groaning and trying desperately to hold back from thrusting up into Al's mouth. Al was patient and slow, building up with determined strokes, never settling to a pattern long enough to let Laurie come close to coming. Nonetheless, Laurie was beginning to lose control before Al started sucking longer, harder, deeper; taking Laurie deep into his throat so that Laurie felt it constrict around him. Up and down and up and down, and fuck, Laurie was coming, his orgasm ripping through him so that his whole body shook with the force of it. Al crouched there, mouth still wrapped around Laurie's cock until it stopped pulsating. Then he let the softening member slide from his mouth, crawled up Laurie's body into his arms, and cried.

Laurie wrapped his arms around Al, holding him close. Half zoned out from coming, he couldn't think of any words so just went for gestures, rocking Al back and forth, first in a comforting way and then, after time, as Al calmed down a bit, and he began to feel Al's erection hardening against him, rocking deliberately into that. Al's cries became heavy breaths, and his fingers started digging into Laurie's skin.

"Fuck. I don't suppose you could..." Al started hesitantly.

Laurie laughed ruefully. "Not after what you just did to me," he said honestly. The only person Laurie ever managed to come with twice in that quick succession was James. He hesitated, sliding a hand round and resting it on Al's arse. "You can fuck me if you want?" he said.

Al stilled in his arms and then sent a startled look up at Laurie. "Did you seriously just say...?"

Laurie swallowed the deep temptation to take the words back. If Al could cope with being assaulted, Laurie could surely cope with being penetrated, even if he never had been before.

"If you want," he said, trying to sound casual.

Al rocked against him a few more times and gave a quiet laugh. "Well. Thanks, but—no. If you can't fuck me, can you at least bring me off?"

"I expect I could manage that." Laurie kissed his forehead. He wasn't used to kissing Al in this way—tenderly, not just to get off. But things were different today. "How do you want it? Hand or mouth?"

"You're not usually this amenable," Al said, an amused tone in his voice.

It was true. Usually, Laurie rather enjoyed *telling* Al what to do, not asking him. "Don't bank on it lasting," Laurie retorted, smiling.

"Hand, then." Al continued to rock against Laurie as he spoke. "Have I ever mentioned what amazing big hands you have? Fucking love your hands."

Laurie lifted one to Al's mouth. "Lick then."

Al could lick hands like he licked cocks: as if there was nothing more he wanted to be doing in the world than what he was. His tongue was wet and tickly against Laurie's palm, the slick saliva coating it quickly. It felt profoundly weird to be having sex with Al without James's participation—James was, as always, so deeply asleep as to be practically comatose—but there were times and moments for worrying about that sort of thing, and this was not it. Laurie lowered his hand to Al's cock, wrapping his strong fingers around him and sliding his damp palm up and down, slowly at first and then faster, his other hand running over Al's chest with the cautiousness Al's bruises required. He rubbed the pad of his thumb across one of Al's nipples and then the other, and Al bucked into his grasp, so Laurie did it again and again until Al was practically fucking himself in Laurie's hand. Even covered in bruises, and white and blotched with shock and lack of sleep, Al was gorgeous like this. Laurie could have watched forever; but it wasn't long until Al was coming, his cock pulsing wetness over Laurie's fingers as he arched his neck back and gasped for breath.

"God, you're gorgeous," Laurie said when Al had come down from his peak, bringing his come-spattered hand to his mouth and licking Al's spunk from it.

"What, bruised and abused?" Al scoffed, only the slightest quaver in his voice making it clear how hard it was for him to joke about it.

Laurie put both his hands on Al's head, forcing him to meet his eyes. "No. Just as you are. As you always are," he said, pressing a kiss to Al's mouth. "Now, are you going to get any sleep, or do you want me to make you some breakfast?"

Al gave a slight shudder at the word sleep. "Don't think I'm ever going to want to sleep again," he confessed.

Laurie smiled and kissed him again. "Breakfast then," he said.

Laurie made a cooked breakfast of eggs, bacon, toast, and mushrooms—one of the few things, as he was wont to say ruefully, which he could reliably make—and ate a bit before standing over Al and making sure that he made a good meal.

"Bully," Al said affably.

"You know it's what James would do, if he was awake."

"If James was awake at this time of the morning, something would be really wrong," Al retorted.

Laurie turned to the washing up to prevent himself saying the obvious: that something was, indeed, truly wrong. James and he had wanted Al to stay the night for some time, but not like this—not like this.

"It's a good job I can make breakfast, then," he said instead.

"Mm. It's not the only thing you can do either." Al's voice was back to its flirty best. "I haven't forgotten this morning, if you have. Your hand on my cock, and—"

"Have I been missing something?" James drawled, wandering into the kitchen in an oversized top and not much else.

"Breakfast, for a start," Al said. "Also, what the fuck are you doing up at this time of day?"

"Missing breakfast, apparently," James retorted.

"As to what else, nothing which wouldn't have been better if you ever bloody woke up," Al added with cheerful bluntness.

"Seconded," Laurie acknowledged, scrubbing the frying pan with vigour, annoyed with himself for flushing. He didn't feel guilty, exactly—not in the circumstances. But he could, perhaps, have done without James walking in at precisely that moment. "D'you want toast, James? Or I can make you some more eggs in a minute after I've cleaned this out."

"At this time of day?" James pulled a face. "Coffee. I'm not doing anything else until I've had coffee."

Al and Laurie both laughed. Laurie had been living with James for more than a year and a half, and Al had been his best friend for fifteen years or so. They both knew that James and mornings were not a match made in heaven. By the time coffee had been made, Laurie had finished the washing up and Al his breakfast, and the three of them ambled into the sitting room and relaxed in the comfortable silence of good friends. (Good friends who were all horrendously underslept, Laurie added wryly to himself.)

The morning passed in such a way, but after lunch Laurie admitted that he needed to get on with some work, and James tried to persuade Al that he might be able to take a nap.

"No thanks," Al said immediately.

James considered him. "I'll come and sit with you," he said.

Al glared. "I don't need company, for fuck's sake."

James grinned. "Okay, I admit it. If we talk in the same room while Laurie's trying to work, he'll probably murder us. Come and chill in the bedroom with me. I'll find you something to wear other than those pyjamas."

"Thanks, love," Laurie said gratefully, combining relief with the knowledge that his tone would persuade Al of James's sincerity.

"If I'm not welcome," Al responded laughingly, shaking his head as he followed James next door.

Laurie nodded at him and turned to his laptop. He wasn't lying—he had masses of work to get through. All the same, he hoped that James could get Al to have a sleep; he suspected that his friend had not got any the night before. Not that Laurie could blame him. He didn't think he would have wanted to shut his eyes in similar circumstances. Feeling slightly sick again, he turned his mind firmly away from the situation and buried himself in the essays. There was a mixed bunch from his first-year students; some would improve massively with the right support, whereas others had probably found their level already, both good and bad. Laurie enjoyed seeing how they progressed as the terms went on. His final year students were different—his courses for them were chosen, not compulsory, so he only dealt with people who had a specific interest in his topics. He began to study them more deeply and was lost to the world.

A couple of hours later, he jerked his head around as James reappeared from the bedroom. "Hey, how's he doing?"

James smiled, his expression tired. "Crashed out, thankfully. I stayed with him for quite a while, but he's been totally under for more than half an hour, so I'm guessing he's good for the moment."

"Good." Laurie shut down his laptop; he'd marked the majority of the essays, and hopefully hadn't been too distracted to make appropriate comments, even though he knew that part of his mind had been with James and Al all the time. He got up and kissed James. "Sorry. I needed to get some stuff done."

"I know."

Laurie hesitated. "About earlier. Me and Al. Did you mind?"

"In the circumstances? No," James said.

Laurie looked at him doubtfully; the words were right, but he wasn't sure how much James meant it. "I don't want to cheat on you. Do anything you don't know about. But..."

"Well. You were hardly having sex behind my back." James gave a brief smile. "I was right there in bed with you, after all."

"Yeah, but still. It felt weird without you," Laurie admitted.

James's smile was more genuine. "I prefer to be involved; I have to admit."

Laurie suppressed his own smile. "Didn't dare wake you, to be honest. You're terrifying when you're woken up."

"Oh, I am not!" James protested indignantly.

"Are too." Laurie kissed the back of James's neck. "Terrifying."

"So. This morning. I gather Al sucked you off."

Apparently, James had done more than just get Al to sleep. Still, it was better this way. Laurie never wanted to have any secrets from James.

"Yeah." He hesitated. "What did he say?"

James shrugged; Laurie felt, rather than saw it. "Nothing much."

"Nothing about why?"

There was a snort from James. "Laurie, really? Al? There needs to be a reason?"

"In this case, yeah." Laurie felt his throat constricting. "He said...fuck..." He buried his head against James's, holding him close.

"What?" James asked sharply.

"Christ, James." Laurie felt his hands clench into fists against James's back. "He said he could... God... Taste them."

He felt James's body stiffen beneath him as if his boyfriend had been turned into a rock. There was a deep, long silence.

"Shit," said James at last.

"Yes."

James sighed and relaxed, and Laurie took advantage and pulled him over to the sofa, collapsing with him. They held each other, and Laurie listened to the sound of James's deep, even breathing.

"Thank you," said James at last.

Laurie wasn't sure what he was being thanked for—the hug, telling James what Al had said...the blow job? If he was being thanked a second time for a blow job he'd fucking loved, he might collapse under the weight of the guilt, so he decided to presume it was one of the other reasons.

"I couldn't..."

"No." James kissed him. Then he grinned. "Did you seriously also offer to let him fuck you?"

Laurie blushed. "Yes." He rested his head on James's shoulder. "Thank god he said no," he said, his voice muffled. "I've only had your finger up there, and—"

"You liked it," James said, half indignant.

"Very much," Laurie admitted readily. "Doesn't mean I want someone's cock up my arse, though." He looked at James's long, slender fingers, very different from...

James gave a sudden little moan, his mind clearly working on very separate lines. "God, I do." He shifted against Laurie. "Up mine, I mean. Please, Laurie. Please. Fuck, I want your cock up my arse right now."

His mouth was open a little way, and his back arched away from Laurie. Laurie took him in with one greedy glance. Fuck, his boyfriend was sexy.

"James," he murmured.

James's fingers dug into his shoulders. He pushed his hips against Laurie's. "Please," he said again.

"You're so hot," Laurie said, kissing him hard. James melted against him as if he wanted nothing else but to meld himself to Laurie's body. Laurie pushed his hips back against James, who met him thrust for thrust. "My pleasure," Laurie said, his hand stroking the side of James's face. He went to put his fingers to James's lips and then stopped, suddenly. "No. Wait."

James's eyes, which had drifted closed as Laurie kissed him, opened. "What?"

A slow smile dawned on Laurie's face. "You do it."

James blinked, opening his eyes properly. "What?" he asked, suddenly less dreamy.

Laurie's look was predatory. "You do it." He slid his hands down James's sides to his hips, stroking over them gently. Licking up the side of James's face to his ear, he murmured, "Finger yourself open for me. Let me watch you. Please, James."

"Fuck." James's face went a bit pink. Nobody could call him shy when it came to Laurie, but there were levels and levels of openness.

"Do it for me, Jamie," Laurie whispered, rocking against his lover. "Please."

James met Laurie's eyes, and slowly, deliberately, began to strip. Top first, and then, standing up and moving away from Laurie, he pushed his trousers and pants off. His cock hung hard and heavy between his legs, and Laurie looked longingly at it, tempted to lean forward and capture it in his mouth. But James's attention was still on him, and Laurie looked back up to meet that dark gaze as James inserted a forefinger in his mouth and began to suck on it, his mouth hollowing round it. Laurie could feel his own cock throbbing, just watching James, and when James took his spit-slickened finger from his lips and slid it behind him, Laurie gave a little groan and pressed his hand hard against his erection.

"Like this, Laurie?" James asked quietly, his gaze never leaving his boyfriend's.

"God yeah, like that," Laurie agreed, wondering how much more of this he could take before he had to give in to the urge to push James chest down on the sofa and fuck him. James gave a little smile and began to suck the middle finger of his left hand, sliding it in and out of his mouth as his right hand worked in and out of his arse. "Jesus, James," Laurie hissed, clutching ever tighter to prevent himself coming even before he'd actually touched James.

James slid onto the end of the sofa, spreading his legs. He moved his hands in front of him between his legs, fucking himself wide open with both of them, his head thrown back but his eyes still meeting Laurie's, searing with heat. And Laurie was so hard that he was going to explode in a second because he'd never, ever seen James do anything like this, and it was quite possibly the most insanely, scorchingly hot thing in the entire universe.

Laurie broke, pushing his own clothes off and wetting his hand to slick his cock before grabbing James hard and kissing him so firmly that he could taste blood when he pulled away.

"Down on the sofa. Now," he said urgently, propelling James round. "God, I'm going to fuck you so hard you'll be screaming, Jamie. On your front. I want to fuck you right through the sofa."

James lay down on his front, looking over his shoulder with a wicked smile on his face. "Like what you see, Laurie?"

"Do I...? Fuck." Laurie was on top of James now, one heavy hand planted in the centre of his back, pushing him down, the other lining himself up behind James's entrance. "Yes," he ground out as he pushed into his lover. "Yes, I like what I fucking see."

James groaned, and Laurie's hand on his back was needed to prevent him from arching up and back. "Want you," he said succinctly.

"You've got me," Laurie assured him, thrusting all the way in.

"Kind of—noticed," James said, the words a bit forced.

Laurie slid a hand round under James to grasp his cock. Then, laying his weight over James, he began to move inside him. Probably he ought to have been going soft and gentle to start with, but James had been looking too fucking gorgeous, and Laurie was too horny to think about doing anything but fucking James as hard and fast as he possibly could. Not that James seemed to be complaining. He might not actually be screaming, but he was moaning out Laurie's name, his cock hot and leaking in Laurie's hand. And Laurie wasn't thinking about anything else but about James; James...the way James felt around his cock; the way James's cock felt in his hand; the noises James was making, the smell of him, the taste of him, the...

"Fuck," Laurie said as he came, his mouth against James's warm, sweaty back, his hand involuntarily clenching around James's cock.

He could hear James moaning louder still, feel the moment when James shook and bucked underneath him, even as every nerve cell in Laurie's body was still fizzing with pleasure.

"James, god," Laurie murmured, kissing his back over and over as he slowly came back to himself.

James was still making little whimpering noises, which were sending aftershocks through Laurie's body, as if there were still some part of him that was continuing to come, even after the first hit of the orgasm was fading. It was so good, so bloody good. James—there was no one, no one ever, like James, Laurie thought, his body flush against his boyfriend's.

"Bloody hell, you're not at it again?" A familiar voice came from behind the sofa as they lay panting on it.

Laurie and James jerked up, almost in tandem, and met Al's half-amused gaze above their heads. James, as Al's best friend, was first to recover from the shock.

"Says—" He cut off suddenly. "—you," James finished weakly, suddenly looking away.

It wasn't exactly difficult to read James's train of thought; common practice was to tease Al unmercifully for his varied and bountiful sex life, but recent circumstances had made that inappropriate. There was, instead, a slightly awkward silence.

"Yeah, well, I'm not in a relationship. It's just unnatural to be together all this time and still fucking like bunnies," Al said after a pause, making a deliberate effort to bridge the moment. "Anyway, that's not the point. I just came to say that I'll be off."

He had dressed himself in some clothes of James's; the trousers were kept up by a tight belt and force of will, Laurie suspected, and Al had had to turn them up at the bottom. He looked young and vulnerable — and definitely not in a fit state to manage by himself.

"What?"

"No, you won't."

The comments came simultaneously from Laurie and James. Laurie, pulling his shirt back on and separating himself from James's body with some slight stickiness, sat back. James got to his feet, apparently unconcerned by the fact he was naked and covered in come. Laurie supposed it wasn't exactly anything Al hadn't seen before. He leant over to get the wipes from the table and gave the sofa a cursory clean as James and Al had it out together.

"You're not going anywhere, thanks," James said firmly to Al. "Not for a few days, anyway."

"I don't live here," Al said mildly, but Laurie could see a slightly hesitant look in his eye, as if Al wasn't particularly keen on heading to his solitary home. "Anyway, I don't want to cramp your style."

"I thought you were just complaining that you *weren't* cramping our style," Laurie said dryly, wiping himself up for good measure.

Al gave a bit of a smile at that. "Yeah, well. Anyway, I need clothes and stuff. You know. Things in my own place. Which isn't here."

James sighed, and after grabbing a wipe from Laurie, shrugged himself into his own clothes. "Yeah, I know, that's skanky of me," he said. "Still. Fine. You want clothes? We'll head over to your house and get you some. And then come back here." He went over to Al and put his arms carefully round him, clearly thinking about his bruises. Laurie couldn't blame him. Al's face looked worse than ever, and Laurie didn't like to think what his body must feel like. "I'm not having you sitting around at your place brooding over stuff. You can brood here, in company."

"I ought…" Al began.

"No, you shouldn't," James said firmly. "You need to be here. With us."

"Sure?" Al's eyes were on Laurie as if he was expecting him to disagree.

"I don't think we're giving you an option," Laurie said casually. "Anyway, I'm taking you both out to dinner, so it's a moot point. Doesn't seem much use going home and then coming out again, though I expect I'll let you get some clothes. No offence, Al, but James's clothes suit him better than they suit you."

"Dinner?" James and Al were both staring at him now.

"Yeah." Laurie smiled. "In case you've forgotten, Al's film just got nominated for an award at the International Film Festival. We've got some celebrating to do. And after that, by the way, Al, you're coming back here. And that's an order."

Al slumped a bit, relief written large over his face. "Shit. Thanks. God, I didn't want to—"

"Then you were a fucking idiot to suggest it," James said ruthlessly. "Come on. We'll get you some stuff, and then I'm coming back and getting in the shower before we go anywhere else."

"If you think I'm taking you out unless you have showered, you're dreaming," Laurie retorted. "And I get first shower when you're out. Go on, then—sooner you're gone, sooner you're back." He stood, stretched, kissed first James and then Al. "See you later."

CHAPTER SIX

The meal was nice, and it was fun to be out, the three of them. They didn't often do this—Al spent so many of his nights out in general that he quite liked staying in with Laurie and James, and James was quite a homebody, rather to his shame. He felt that as a twenty-four-year-old bloke he ought to enjoy being out getting pissed, but in truth he was happiest sitting at home in the flat with some music on, a glass of wine, and Laurie's arms around him. Which suited Laurie very nicely as well. After all, Laurie himself had been an undergraduate who'd been happier hanging around at Gillie and Terry's house with their young son and his best friend than going out partying. He wasn't exactly a dirty stop-out by nature either. Laurie, however, hadn't had a friend like Al driving home the difference between them. It didn't bother Al in the slightest, mind; it was only James who was a little self-conscious about his natural instincts.

Nonetheless, as a one-off, it was enormous fun to be out together, teasing Al with bigger and more expansive compliments about his film-making skills. In return, Al was threatening to announce to the international film community that the guitarist at the beginning and end of the film was James, to James's absolute horror, and Laurie promised that he would use the film as proof of all that was good and beautiful in short film-making, which had Al and James combining to tell him that it would be a safe way to find himself out of a job. Laurie had a brief guilty moment remembering the last way he'd nearly found himself out of a job and was suddenly silent.

They'd ambled home again around 10:00 p.m., and once more all shacked up in Laurie and James's bed, sharing the sort of kisses and cuddles that Al generally made rude comments about but that just at the moment seemed to be precisely what he needed.

"I've got work tomorrow," Al said, lying with his head on Laurie's shoulder and James's arm flung over his back.

"Don't go," said James immediately. "Phone in sick." He propped himself up on one elbow and looked at Al, whose bruises were turning interesting shades of purple and blue by now. "It's perfectly true. You're not fit enough to be anywhere."

Sometimes James was very like his mother, Laurie thought tenderly. He had a maternal streak a yard wide, though he was usually very careful to conceal it.

Al sighed. "Can't do that. Fen's short-staffed at the moment. She usually covers absence, but she's already going to be in. It's not 'til 2:00 p.m. anyway. Don't know why I mentioned it, really. It just came to mind."

"When are you working 'til?" Laurie asked.

He felt Al tense beside him. "Ten."

"I don't care," said James stubbornly. "If you're not well enough, you're not well enough."

"I'll be fine."

"I'll meet you afterwards," said Laurie abruptly.

James, who had been about to say something else, was suddenly silent as if he had only just realised why Al was concerned.

"No one will—" Al began.

"No," said Laurie simply, "they won't. And I'll meet you afterwards."

"You're very—"

"Sensible."

Al smiled into his shoulder. "Bossy, I was going to say."

"Settle on determined?" James suggested. "I still think you shouldn't go, but I can see you're going to take about as much notice of me as you usually do."

"James," Al said, wounded, "I am your devoted...your devoted..."

"My devoted liar is what you are," James said roughly, but he nuzzled his head against Al's as he slid down from his elbow again. "Now, let's see if we can't get some more sleep than we did last night."

"You, at least," Al agreed. "You're awful without enough sleep."

Laurie gave a stifled snort of laughter. James mumbled something extremely rude under his breath. They tried to sleep.

☆☆☆

It was clear in the morning that Al hadn't slept much better than the night before. He acknowledged as much but shrugged it off.

"Sometimes when I'm filming, I have weeks like this," he said coolly.

"Or when you're fucking," James retorted, having clearly decided that one day without commenting on Al's sex life was more than enough. He was probably right, Laurie thought—*not* mentioning it was more jarring, bringing Al's assault more obviously to mind.

"Or then," Al agreed. "We're allowed to mention that again, then?"

Laurie grinned. Apparently Al agreed.

James gave an indignant snort. "Here I was, aiming for tact and things of that sort, and what gratitude do I get?"

Al looked serious for a moment. "I am grateful to both of you," he said quietly. "Probably haven't said that enough."

"More than enough," Laurie said quickly. "We haven't done anything."

Not even warned him that someone was threatening him. Laurie's guilt was getting the better of him. He had a feeling that he needed to tell James, but he had a sickening feeling that James would be angry. Furious. If James blamed him for Al getting assaulted, would he leave him? And what the hell would James say if he knew he'd got drunk and started making threats himself? Laurie shook his head a little to clear away the worst of the thoughts in time to hear James add, "Except not mention your sex life for more than twenty-four hours and look at the gratitude I got for that."

Laurie had a feeling that James knew something was up with him, however. He hadn't said anything in front of Al—they were all keeping a teasing, light-hearted front up this morning—but when Al had left for work, Laurie wasn't entirely surprised when James turned to him. Ostensibly, Laurie was making coffee; in fact, he was pacing up and down the kitchen, wondering what he should say to James and what he emphatically should not. The trouble was, the more he thought about it, the more confused he got and the worse he felt about everything. In a way, it was a relief when James tackled him, sitting down at the kitchen table and leaning his arms on the back of the chair, staring at Laurie over the top of it.

"You've been prowling up and down half the weekend," James said. "Are you going to tell me what's on your mind—apart from the obvious?"

Laurie cast him a troubled look. "It's..."

"Is it about the police?" James asked. "I agree with you Al should call them, but—"

"No. It's not that." Laurie sighed. "I'm just...worried you're going to kill me," he said tightly.

There was a hard look in James's eyes. "Unless you were out on Friday night with a knife in your hand, no, I don't think I'm going to kill you." He gave a brief smile. "Which you weren't, as you were having dinner with me. So, what?"

Laurie was pacing again. He made a conscious effort to stop himself. "You know the other week when I was out with the department?" he said slowly.

"What, when you got into a bit of an argument with a student?" James said.

Laurie nodded. "Thing is, I didn't exactly tell you all of it," he confessed.

"Ok-aay," said James, looking at him.

Shorn of pacing about, Laurie started to tap his fingers against his thigh very fast. "Al's name was mentioned," he said, getting the words out quickly before he could think better of it.

"What?" demanded James, sharply.

Laurie swallowed. "Not just homophobic threats, but with Al's name attached. And if I'd had the goddamn courage to tell you about it, this might not have happened." He couldn't meet James's eye, scared of what he'd see there. "I just...didn't think it was *real*, not actually meaning anything. And besides..." He trailed off.

"Why didn't you tell me?"

"I was..." Laurie flapped a hand helplessly, sweating a bit under James's questioning. "Embarrassed. How was I supposed to come home and tell you what someone had been saying about Al? I didn't want to repeat it. Still don't. And...um..."

"There's more," James said, his voice cold and clear.

Laurie's head dropped, and he could feel himself flushing. "I did something I wasn't very proud of," he muttered. "Didn't want to tell you about it."

He sensed, rather than saw, James get to his feet. He'd known James would blame him—he blamed himself. Laurie felt suddenly sick.

"What?" James asked, tone very hard and angry.

"I er...I er... Shit," said Laurie, turning away, terrified of what he might see in James's face if he looked. "I had my hand on his wrist, and I think...I think I threatened to break his arm if he ever said anything about Al again. Possibly both his arms. I'm not sure."

He waited for James to explode. Unexpectedly, his boyfriend laughed softly. Laurie was so shocked, he turned around.

"Well," James said, and a smile tugged at the corner of his mouth as he went over to Laurie and wound an arm around his neck, "that is unexpected. You're right."

"I don't... You're not... I thought you'd be furious."

"What, because you defended Al?" James asked, raising an eyebrow. "Geez, Laur, the way you were going on, I thought you'd joined in or something. Or at any rate pretended not to know him."

"What the hell?" snapped Laurie, caught on the raw by this.

"Hey, don't sound so offended. It was only because you were so unwilling to tell me," James said, kissing his neck.

It was hard to go on being offended with James kissing his neck. "But... Christ, James, I can't go round threatening my students," Laurie said, leaning his head against James's. It dropped a bit further. "And I'm so sorry I didn't tell you. God, I don't know what I was thinking. I—didn't want Al to know people were saying shit about him, and then this happened, and I keep wondering whether I could've stopped it if I'd told you, if he'd known."

James held him close. "Enough of this blame thing. We've got Al blaming himself for being Al, and you blaming yourself for not taking more notice of one stupid comment in a pub. The people to blame are the bastards who did this to him. You and Al have done nothing wrong."

"Except threaten a student," Laurie muttered guiltily into James's hair.

James huffed a laugh. "I wish I'd seen it," he confessed. "Serve the bastard right, by the way, but I find it quite hard to imagine you making threats."

"I was angry," Laurie said sheepishly. "And it was Al."

James stilled and looked up at Laurie. "Ah, there's the thing, isn't it?" he said, smiling lovingly at Laurie. "It was Al."

Laurie nodded, closing his arms round James even more firmly. "I know I say he's a brat," he said, "but he's our brat, Jamie. I won't have people hurting him."

"I love you so much," James whispered. "Love you more for this."

"He's ours," Laurie said again. "Not in the same way that I'm yours and you're mine. That's different. But Al..."

"Yeah. I know." James kissed him again. "Wasn't sure you did, though."

"Been thinking." Laurie went on, eyeing James.

"Mm-hmm?" James was busy kissing Laurie's neck, which was very distracting, but now that Laurie had finally started getting some of this stuff out, he wanted to finish.

"If I moved all my film crap out of the spare room and into the sitting room," Laurie said tentatively, "it's quite a big room in there. Big enough that..."

"Are you saying what I think you're saying?" James said, looking up from his self-appointed task.

"It's just..."

"Al," said James.

Laurie nodded. "He could...entertain in there, if he gave us a bit of warning. It's big enough, and it has a decent-sized bed under all the films and such, and, well...I don't like the thought of him going back to an empty house and no one knowing if he's turned up or not, or... I'm fussing, aren't I?"

"No more than I've been," James admitted. "I couldn't suggest...that...but... I've just been worried that they'll've made him scared to be Al. Go out, flirt, shag—god, Laurie, it's not like he's been hurting anyone. He's not been pretending or lying to people. He's never pretended about anything." His voice broke a little. "He's my best friend, and...and..."

"And a bit more than that even," Laurie agreed. "Our Al."

"Yeah," said James, with a sigh. "I just want him safe and happy. I won't let them take that away from him, Laurie."

"Me neither. So," Laurie added questioningly, "if he had somewhere safe to—to be Al, where we could look after him a bit. Not get in his way, interfere at all," he added hastily. "Just, you know." James nodded from within his arms. "What do you think?"

"I think if he says no, I'll move him in myself," James said grimly. "You're sure you don't mind someone else living here with us?"

"I'm sure I'd mind someone else living here with us," said Laurie, "but this isn't someone else. It's Al. God, I sound like I'm in love with the guy."

"Are you?" asked James shrewdly.

Laurie caught his eye. "Maybe? A little? Not in the same way I'm in love with you, but there's something. You know. You've got it too—you're no better than I am."

"No," agreed James. "You're right, though, it's nothing like us. And for the record, if you ever even consider shagging around, I'll dismember you piece by tiny piece. But still, Al…"

"Yes, that's precisely it." Laurie grinned. "Same goes for you, incidentally. I'm the sort of person who makes threats now, remember."

James laughed, sounding happier than he had since the moment Al turned up thirty-eight hours earlier. "Fuck. Such a relief. So what do we do now?"

"First," said Laurie firmly, "I'm taking you back to bed and reminding you quite how important you are to me. After that, we've got a few hundred films to move…"

CHAPTER SEVEN

It was hard physical work moving the DVDs and the bookcases on which they abided, and more than once before they finished, James muttered dark invectives about Laurie and his film-hoarding habits. Both men were sweating and exhausted by the time everything had been moved from the spare room, and the time was ticking on. But the house was in order again when Laurie left to go and meet Al from work, and James had collapsed on the sofa in a dramatic fashion more suited to his best friend, declaring that he was never getting up again. Laurie kissed him and left.

It was still early when he arrived at the wine shop—about ten to ten. Laurie took a quick look in and saw that Al and his boss, Fenella, were sorting out the shop. Counting money from the till. Laurie knew from experience that six-foot-something blokes going into a shop and hanging around doing nothing weren't always welcome at such moments, and god knew he didn't want to embarrass Al by explaining he'd come to pick him up from work. He wondered what Al had told Fen—he'd have had to tell her something to explain the fact that half his face was deep purplish-red and bruised, but Laurie hadn't liked to mention that before Al went to work. It was hardly as if Al wasn't aware of the way he currently looked, after all. Or felt. Al had sheepishly admitted that he was downing painkillers every four hours like they were sweets, after James had found him sneaking into the kitchen and looking around cautiously before filling a glass. Laurie hadn't quite liked to ask James what the hell he'd *thought* Al was doing. From the sound of it, James had been controlling a huge amount of pent-up paranoia. Anyway, the shame with which Al had admitted to needing pain control had been worthy of a better cause. Pain wasn't, as Laurie had reminded Al firmly, a character flaw.

Anyhow, Laurie hung around outside, a little distance from the shop. He was grateful that it was a decent evening, even despite the cold. Finally, he heard the door begin to open and walked towards it.

"Don't stay, Al. I can manage from here," Fen called.

"Yeah, okay." Al's voice sounded a little strained, and Laurie moved more swiftly towards him, unwilling to let him hang around alone on the doorstep.

"Hey," he said, tapping Al gently on the shoulder as he came up to him.

"Laurie!" Al let go of the shop door and clutched his chest in an age-old gesture of shock. "God, you scared the bejesus out of me."

"Hell. Sorry," Laurie apologised. Appearing out of the darkness at someone who got attacked a couple of days earlier by a group of people appearing out of the darkness. Nice one, Laurie, he castigated himself mentally. "I didn't want to hang around in the shop looking like some sinister spectre at the feast in case your boss didn't appreciate it," he explained guiltily. "But I should've thought. Sorry."

Al gave a weak grin. "No, you're right. Fen would probably not have wanted you standing about watching her cash up. I'm just a bit twitchy. Sorry, yourself."

"I feel like an idiot," Laurie apologised.

"Nothing new there, then," Al said, his grin widening. Then he sobered up, touching Laurie's arm. "Seriously, though, thanks for this. Meeting me, I mean. Didn't realise how much of a fucking wuss I was until it came to going out, and it was dark, and..."

Laurie bit his lip. Bastards. He felt the now-familiar wave of anger wash over him. So much for being a peaceable sort of chap. Laurie would quite happily have committed murder at the moment, given the right targets. He pulled Al into a one-armed hug.

"Not a problem. You'd do the same for me."

Al looked at him, his strange green eyes lit by the street light above them. "Yes, I would," he said quietly. "I'm glad you know that."

Laurie felt his cheeks flush, despite the cold. He hadn't known, not really. If he'd thought about it, he'd have presumed that Al liked him well enough—but probably more as James's boyfriend, not for himself particularly. His own feelings for Al were one thing (and he was slightly embarrassed about his level of protectiveness, not to mention love, towards the younger man), but he had no thought that they were reciprocated, and he hadn't been unduly bothered by that. They didn't have that sort of relationship. But there was something simple and genuine in Al's response that was touching. It wasn't the normal, teasing young man who Laurie usually knew. Laurie mumbled something incoherent and left his arm around Al's shoulders as they walked towards home. James was too tall to hold like this; Laurie's hand always fell across his back and rounded his waist on the far side. But Al was five or six inches shorter than Laurie, and Laurie's arm slipped around his shoulders quite comfortably.

"What did Fen say—about your face?" Laurie asked.

Al shrugged. "Told her I got in a fight."

Laurie raised an eyebrow. Of all the people to get in a fight, Al was one of the least likely. Al stared at his and Laurie's feet.

"Told her she should've seen the other guy," he mumbled. "Wasn't true. They were fine."

"They were a 'they'," Laurie said, trying not to sound as angry as he felt. "With a knife."

Al shrugged. It was such a familiar gesture, but this time Laurie's arm was around Al, so he could feel it go through him. It seemed as if he could also feel the self-hatred Al was experiencing, too. It burnt, and Laurie felt helpless to do anything about it.

"Yeah," Al said, at last. There was a silence. Then, "Laurie," he said.

"Uh-huh?"

"I think I'm ready to tell the police now."

Laurie could feel Al tense as he said the words; it was not going to be an easy experience for him, Laurie knew.

"You're bloody brave."

Al huffed, a little puff of cold air escaping from his lips. "Hardly," he said. "Think I'm being anything but." He stopped walking, shivering a little. "Thought how I'd feel if they did it to Fen. To someone else." He leaned his head against Laurie's arm. "I have to, don't I?"

"No," Laurie said quietly. "You don't. But you will, because you're brave. Because you're you. Because you're thinking about someone else two days after you—"

"Yeah," said Al, cutting him off quickly. He hadn't let them say the word—not Laurie, not James, definitely not himself. "I was shit. But—"

It was Laurie's turn to cut Al off. "No, you weren't. And no, you aren't." There were moments when one-armed hugs didn't cut it. Laurie pulled Al close in against him, holding him as tightly as possible without pressing against him too painfully. No need to remind Al of all the bits of him that hurt in quite so physical a fashion. "You're being incredible, all right?" Laurie whispered in Al's ear. "Don't think otherwise."

"Going to carry on hugging me like this?" Al asked, sounding a bit happier. "Because you're having a decent effect on my ego." He gave a little wriggle, pushing himself up against Laurie. "More than my ego," he added thoughtfully.

A warm Al pushed up against him was rather too good for a public street, Laurie thought. He said as much to Al, who laughed.

"Better get me home then," he said, letting go of Laurie with faint reluctance. "Talk to you and James about the police. Do I call 'em from home, or go in and see them, or...? I dunno."

"I kept your clothes separate," Laurie said. "Just in case. They'll probably tell you that you should've gone in immediately, but I can tell them to fuck off for you if you want."

Al made a sound that was trying to be a laugh. "I'm not sure you're helping entirely, but I appreciate the offer. Oh well. But like I say, the blokes who did it to me might do it to someone else. Not sure I can live with that thought. Don't want to feel responsible."

"Yeah, I know that one," Laurie muttered guiltily. He looked away from Al. "Sorry. Nothing important. But I think you're right, and it will be good just to have got it done. Come on."

It was past 10:30 p.m. when they got home, and Laurie could tell from the expression on James's face that he'd just been beginning to get a little bit anxious. He didn't think Al had noticed, but Laurie knew that James was more inclined to worry than he liked to let on.

"Hey, love," he said, giving James a kiss.

"What bloody time do you call this?" James grumbled, the nearest he'd get to admitting he'd been concerned.

Al looked at his watch. "About ten thirty-two, I should think. It's—hey, what have you been doing in here?"

He stared around at the room, which looked (Laurie had to admit it) rather more crowded with the large Blu-ray and DVD collection slotted neatly into bookcases across the back wall.

"Moving things around," James said casually. "What do you think?"

"That you've got an insane amount of films." Al's voice was almost awed as he went over towards the rows.

"What, and you haven't?" Laurie demanded cynically.

Al turned to him, his hands wide apart. "Laurie, what can I say? I'm a modern man. I stream things. I don't have DVDs. Not like this, anyway." He took another good look. "I don't think *anyone* has disks quite like this," he added. "How many?"

"Four hundred and sixty-nine," said James, in the grim voice of someone who had moved them.

"What've you brought them all out here for, though?" Al asked.

Laurie and James exchanged a look. They had known that the subject would have to be brought up, but they still didn't really know how to go about it.

"Ah," said James.

"Well," said Laurie.

"Now you ask..." James said. "We were clearing out the other room, if you must know."

"What, the junk hole?" Al asked in disbelief. "I thought that room was a myth!"

"What do you mean, 'the junk hole'?" Laurie asked.

Al had the grace to blush. "Um...oops. Sorry. I've always kind of called it that to myself because no one's ever allowed in there, and I just presumed that it was such a disaster you shut the door and wouldn't let anyone in, in case the whole lot fell down on their heads."

James and Laurie were open-mouthed in disbelief and outrage. Al shifted awkwardly from one foot to another.

"Did he just..." Laurie said to James, his voice incredulous.

James nodded. Al held up his hands.

"Shit. God, can we just pretend I didn't say that? Come on, you're being nice to me and everything." He paused for a second but went on as if he couldn't help himself. "But...why have you moved them out of there?"

"Want to look?" Laurie asked.

"Want? I'm gagging for it," Al assured him.

James pushed open the door, and Al stopped in the doorway.

The room looked good. The room, Laurie thought, looked very good. Whilst Laurie had been out getting Al, despite his protestations about never moving again, James had in fact made up the double bed with clean sheets and a duvet cover. The tall, thin cupboard against the wall was still full of Laurie's junk, but the wardrobe—which James flung open—was empty; the room looked enormous with the boxes of goodness-knows-what pushed into the built-in cupboards elsewhere in the house. If he were honest, Laurie was feeling quite embarrassed that they'd been wasting this room all that time. On the other hand, it did mean that it was just waiting for someone to fill it. Someone like Al.

No, not 'someone like Al'. Al.

"Bloody hell," Al said. "This has been here all along? You haven't just magicked it up somehow?"

"It's the 'Room of Requirement'," said James, which meant very little to Laurie but apparently worked for Al.

"Oh yeah?" he said. "What's the requirement?"

"Space for you," James said simply.

Al turned to him, a slight frown on his face. "Huh?"

"A room for you."

"Sorry. Didn't realise I was taking up that much room," Al apologised. "I can go home, though. You didn't need to disinter the jun—the spare room, you know."

"No!" James clutched his head. "We didn't mean that. I mean..."

"We want you to stay," Laurie finished simply.

"Just...not in your bed. Which is fair enough, obviously," Al said hastily. "I mean, it's not like—"

"Shut up!" roared James, unexpectedly loudly. "Um, sorry."

"We want you to live here," Laurie explained. "With us." There was a half thought in the back of his mind as he finished speaking, which he couldn't quite articulate yet. A bad feeling. There was no reason for it—Al was just looking puzzled, but somehow...something seemed off. He shook his head a little, trying to clear his mind.

"With your own room," James added, still looking embarrassed at having yelled. "But, you know, just—stay."

"What?"

"Stay here," said James. Laurie, looking at him, saw how vulnerable he looked, how much he needed Al to be here—to know his best friend was safe. But somehow that vulnerability didn't translate to his speech, which came out almost as an instruction, sharp and authoritative.

"You're joking. Stop taking the piss."

"I'm not taking the piss," James said, the frustration in his voice mounting. "It's not that bloody difficult. Just move in."

"No," said Al baldly. He glared at the pair of them. "I'm not a freaking charity case."

"Suit yourself," said Laurie, leaning against the door frame, the half thoughts rising once more to the surface. He knew how James would feel, hearing him say that, but he knew Al of old. More opposition would drive their lover to ever-increasing stubbornness, which was the last thing they needed right now.

James looked at him furiously as if he'd been betrayed. "Laurie!" He turned to Al. "Al!"

"I don't," said Al, through gritted teeth, "need babysitters."

"We never said you did," James protested.

"Come off it, James," Al said, the mulish expression still on his face, "you've never asked me to stay before. Just because I—oh fuck it," he snapped out, "just because I got *raped* doesn't mean I'm going to make a bloody habit of it."

"I know," said James, his anger softening in the face of Al's experience. "I know. It's just—"

"I don't need you feeling sorry for me all the time. I'll be fine. I've been a bit shit for a couple of days, granted—"

"No, you haven't," interrupted James quickly.

"—but I'm just fine. Jesus, James, I'm mortified enough already without you feeling like you need to start taking over my life for me."

"It's not like that."

Laurie knew that James was close to tears. He had a horrible feeling that Al was, too. All in all, this conversation was emphatically not going to plan. He'd half realised, the moment they began to bring the subject up, how Al would take it. And it was so bloody difficult, on the back of everything that had happened, to start explaining to Al just how important he was to them—just how much he mattered—without it sounding like a pathetic way of reassuring someone who needed no such reassurance in the first place, for goodness sake. Laurie didn't want Al here for Al's sake, he admitted to himself. He wanted him here for Laurie's sake, and James's. They needed Al, not the other way around. Not in a possessive way, but because the thought of anything happening to him was too horrific even to consider. Al might cope with anything that life threw at him—indeed, he probably would—but Laurie wasn't sure that he and James could do so.

"No?" demanded Al. The level of anger, Laurie thought suddenly, was out of proportion to the suggestion: as if Al was tempted and then furious with himself for wanting to stay. As well he might be if he didn't believe that the other two truly wanted him. "Then what is it like?"

"It doesn't have to be forever," Laurie said, using his new suspicion to rejoin the fray—clearly to the surprise of both Al and James. "Just for a few months." If he stayed for a bit, maybe they could persuade Al that they really wanted him long-term. Forever, in fact. Laurie moved over to stand behind James and wrapped his arms around him. "For James's sake, Al. He's a terrible worrywart, you know. He gets horribly anxious about things, and then he's hell to live with. If you don't stay, at least for a bit, he'll spend all his time fussing about you. He won't be able to think about anything else. And you don't want to destroy James's peace of mind utterly, do you?"

"Laurie," James hissed indignantly, making a half-hearted struggle to free himself from Laurie's grip, "you're outrageous."

"No," Al corrected, a faint smile drifting over his face for the first time since the conversation had started, "merely manipulative. *Very* manipulative."

Laurie looked Al straight in the eyes. "Even if it's true?"

James fought more seriously to escape at this, but Laurie made the most of his strength and continued to hold him tightly corralled against his body. He wished he could communicate what he was thinking to his lover, who only knew that his closest guarded secret was, in fact, being given away. Laurie wondered whether James realised that Al didn't believe it...yet.

"It's..." James started to object, but Laurie kissed his neck.

"What? It's not true? Liar," he said quietly, though loud enough for Al to hear.

James couldn't help guilty colour flooding his cheeks. "Shut up, Laurie."

Al looked at the pair of them steadily. Laurie took a deep breath.

"If you're worried we'll cramp your style," he said, "we won't. Bring home who you like—however many of 'em you like. Warn us in advance if possible, but we're quite capable of keeping out of the way if necessary, and this room's plenty big enough for all sorts of things. We won't even come running if we hear you shouting 'no' loudly, in case it's a scene."

It was Al's turn to blush at this explicit reference to his sex life. "I can't believe you just said that," he said, mouth dropping open, looking at Laurie as if at a new person.

Laurie shrugged, mildly amused that *he* had the ability to embarrass *Al* when it came to sex. "Reckon if you needed us, you could probably manage our names," he said simply. "They're not that difficult. And if you're worried you'll cramp our style, don't be. You won't." He grinned at Al. "On the other hand, if you're worried you *won't* cramp our style, you might have more of a problem. I'm not going to stop kissing Jamie, even for you." He proved the point by running his tongue around the edge of James's ear, making James groan and lean back into him.

"I think you're embarrassing him," James said, his eyes closed and his head lolling back against Laurie's shoulder.

"To be fair, I think I'm embarrassing all of us," Laurie said honestly. He met Al's gaze again. "There's one other thing, though."

Al was beginning to look resigned to his fate. "Go on. Tell me."

"Ah," said Laurie. "See, this is the bit where I really do get embarrassed. I'm not good at this sort of thing. But the thing is that James and me, we..."

"I'm really not sure I need to know," Al said hurriedly, and Laurie laughed.

"Nothing like that," he said. "Thing is, we...well, hell; this is awkward. We rather love you, Al."

"Beg your pardon?" Al's eyes narrowed as if he was suspecting a trick.

"James?" Laurie prompted, basely bottling out and leaving his boyfriend to do the work.

"Fuck you, Laurie," James said amiably.

"I thought no one did," Al put in wickedly.

James's eyes glinted. "He gave you the chance. Take a bloody hint, Al. Possibly he's keener on you than he likes to admit."

Al snorted. "And possibly pigs can fly."

Laurie let go of James gently and went over to Al. Sliding an arm around him, he directed him round and pointed a finger at the ceiling.

"See that?" he asked.

Al looked up, bewildered. "What?"

"Flying pig," Laurie said. He kissed Al lightly on the cheek. "Maybe you ought to listen to your best friend sometimes. And maybe he's more than a best friend. Think about that."

"You're taking the piss," Al said.

Laurie laughed. "About the airborne porcine, maybe. About the rest, not so much. It's okay. I think I'm done embarrassing us all for tonight. I'm sure there are better things we could be doing."

Al's eyes glinted. "We-ell," he started slowly. "If I'm going to be staying here for a while, it strikes me that the bed may need christening. As it were." He glanced up at Laurie. "Start as you mean to go on, after all. Or start as you clearly think I mean to go on, anyway."

"Okay." Laurie strolled over to the bed and sat down on it. "James?" he asked.

James was beginning to smile. Laurie reserved hope that he might someday be forgiven for telling Al how worried James got about things. It didn't suit the cool image of himself that James liked to portray. Laurie hadn't the heart to tell him that Al probably knew him better than that anyway. James moved towards the bed, collecting Al in one arm on his way over, and toppling him onto the crisp, clean sheets.

"How are you doing, Al?" Laurie asked, wincing again at the sight of Al's bruises as he carefully removed his shirt.

Al grinned a little ruefully. "I wouldn't say this often," he said, "but be gentle with me, guys, yeah?"

James stroked a hand over him, sensitive fingers brushing gently against Al's skin. "We will," he promised.

"Not my most romantic statement ever. Or sexiest," Al admitted.

"I happen to find sex considerably sexier when my lover isn't screaming in pain," Laurie said practically. "Well," he added as an afterthought, "unless that's what turns him on, obviously."

"Yes," said Al, looking suspiciously at him. "You seem to know much too much about things that I'd never have expected. How do... Wait, on second thoughts, I think I'd rather not know."

Laurie chuckled. "Our Al, prudish?"

"Jamie clearly has hidden depths."

"Excuse me," James interrupted. "I'm not sure how I got dragged into this conversation. I'm beginning to think I'm the only normal one among us."

"Says the person who suggested a threesome in the first place," said Laurie lazily.

"People harp on about one minor moment," James retorted. "However, that's not the point at the moment."

"No," agreed Laurie. "The point is that we've got to be gentle with Al here, just for tonight."

Suddenly, there was a mischievous glint in James's eyes, which Laurie recognised. "We'll be gentle," James assured Al again. He exchanged a glance with Laurie, and Laurie realised that he knew precisely what was going through James's mind.

"Very gentle," he agreed, ably assisting his boyfriend. "Just lie back, Al, and we'll look after you. Very, very gently."

"Why don't I trust you?" said Al, a small smile on his lips.

"Al, your mistrust pains me. It really does," James said, shaking his head. He kissed Al lightly on the lips.

Laurie unbuttoned Al's trousers and slid them off him slowly with his boxers. "You could take your top off as well, James," he commented. "For my sake, if nothing else."

"I will if you will."

Topless, the two men returned their attention to Al, who was lying on the bed dressed only in some socks, which Laurie was peeling off his feet. James, lying beside Al, began to kiss him: chaste, soft kisses, his hands stroking Al's face and rubbing little circles on his shoulders. Laurie, having removed Al's socks, turned his attention to Al's feet, nuzzling them with his face before sucking Al's toes into his mouth, one by one, lapping his tongue around them.

"Mmmph," said Al, making a half-hearted effort to twitch his foot away from Laurie's ministrations.

"Shh," said James reassuringly, kissing his neck and running his hands down Al's arms. "We'll look after you."

Laurie laid a line of kisses across Al's instep, and the younger man squealed and kicked out in earnest. "Ticklish," he grumbled accusingly at Laurie, who laughed and did it again, this time holding his leg down firmly to prevent another kick. "Bastard," Al muttered, but James went back to kissing his mouth—longer kisses now, but still so very, very gentle, and he sighed, wrapping his arms around James in return.

Laurie moved on to his ankles and then up to the backs of his knees—Al was ticklish there, too, it seemed—his mouth trailed higher as James's hands trailed lower, fingers skimming across Al's flat, pale, and bruised belly in a repetitive motion. Al was trying to rock his body, increase the pressure against it, but Laurie and James were able to keep him still between them. His hands were grabbing more tightly onto James's back now. If it weren't for the fact that he bit his nails, they would probably have been digging into James's skin, but as it was, they were just touching the surface.

"Get on with it," he whined.

Laurie looked up, apparently hurt. "We're being gentle, Al," he protested innocently.

"Just as you asked," James added.

"I really hate you both," Al complained, his cock hard and beginning to leak pre-come from the tip, even without having been touched.

"No you don't," James whispered, licking round his ear and putting one finger—just one finger—to the underside of Al's cock for a second. It bobbed and jerked under the touch, and James laughed. "You really don't," he said, nibbling the shell of Al's ear.

"I really do."

Laurie was kissing Al's thighs, working his way from the outside to the inside, still ensuring that none of the motions brought him anywhere near Al's cock. Al began to make little noises of protest, trying to reach his own hands down to touch himself, but James caught Al's fingers in his own and held onto them.

"Why, what do you want, Al?" Laurie asked.

Al seethed. "You know damn well what I want."

"I want to hear you say it."

Laurie returned to Al's thighs, running his tongue down the insides, nipping the flesh gently where there wasn't a bruise, lapping over the skin where there was.

"Fuck," Al swore. "I want you to *touch my cock*, all right?"

"Oh," said James, sounding surprised. "So that's what he wants."

"Mm. Still something missing, though," Laurie said, his mouth so close that he knew that Al could feel the warm breath against his erection. "A word."

"So there is," agreed James, swiping his mouth across one of Al's nipples unexpectedly, making Al give out a smothered yelp, jerking his hips hard forwards.

Laurie and James ignored this, continuing their slow, intimate exploration of his body. Al was literally writhing now.

"The magic word, Al," Laurie reminded him.

Al looked as if he would have loved to say a great number of words, all extremely impolite, to Laurie. But at the same time, he was too desperate to do so right now. The need to be touched was overriding all other impulses.

"Please," he hissed reluctantly.

"Sorry, didn't hear that," Laurie said wickedly.

Al broke. "Please. Please, please, please. Oh god, I need..."

Laurie moved his mouth a few inches upwards and captured the head of Al's cock in his mouth. Al cried out, the last of his control leaving him as he groaned over and over while Laurie moved his warm wet lips up and down Al's shaft. James continued to lick and kiss and nibble all of Al's upper body. Laurie had gone down on Al before, and he knew what the young man liked. It took only a few minutes before Al was pulsing in his mouth, warm come coating Laurie's mouth and throat. He took it all, revelling in the salt-bitter taste of Al. When Al was finished, Laurie wriggled round to lie next to him.

"See?" he said. "We can do gentle."

"We certainly can," James agreed. He leaned forward to kiss Laurie hard. "Mm, you taste good," he said.

"I think you mean Al does," Laurie replied.

"God, and you two are still half dressed. How embarrassing," Al said, but his tone could not quite manage embarrassed. Laurie knew from his own past experiences that it was difficult to sound bad directly after a decent (or should that be indecent?) orgasm.

"I think he wants you to take your trousers off, Jamie," he commented. He grinned. "I do, anyway."

James smiled at him. "Remember what I said about tops?" he asked.

I will if you will. Ah, okay then.

"What? Are you two going to fuck in front of me?" Al asked. It didn't sound like an objection.

"Maybe," James said.

"Depends how long your recovery period is," Laurie added suggestively, shrugging the rest of his clothes off and then snogging Al as he waited for James to do the same. He usually liked watching James undress, but tonight was about Al and trying to make him realise how very, very welcome he was here. How much he belonged with James and Laurie.

"Oh," said Al, thoughtfully. "Now, *that* I like the thought of."

"Don't get me wrong," said Laurie, returning his eyes to James appreciatively. "I'm always happy to have sex with James."

"I'd noticed," Al put in dryly.

"Still, as you're here..." Laurie trailed off invitingly.

"Seems foolish not to make the most of it," James agreed, leaning across Al to kiss Laurie passionately.

"Bloody hell, if I get to watch you snog like that, I'll be ready in minutes," Al said, reaching up both hands and running one down each of his lovers.

Laurie and James didn't respond, too busy rediscovering each other. It seemed not to matter how many times Laurie kissed James. Every time, it left him wanting and desperate, aching to push himself up against his lover and frot against him madly until James was begging him to fuck him. James's arms pulled him closer, closer. Al was not quite forgotten, but Laurie was remembering once again how little he needed except James like this, touching him. Kissing him. Wanting him.

Al continued to stroke them, however; his gestures steadily more intimate. He had a hand on Laurie's arse, on James's thigh. Sliding the bitten tips of his nails across Laurie's buttocks. Curving round to take James's cock in his hand. James took his mouth away from Laurie's to take a big unexpected breath, and Laurie looked down at Al, amusement in his eyes.

"Didn't take you long, then," he commented.

"Not with you two going at it right across me," Al said. He moved his other hand from Laurie's arse and grasped Laurie's cock as well, stroking them both in time.

James took a hissed breath. "Fuck, Al."

"I was rather hoping so," Al agreed mischievously.

He continued to stroke, and Laurie, looking down, saw James's hand go to Al's cock, already half hard again. Then James leant down and kissed Al.

"Want me to fuck you, then?" he asked, lying carefully on top of his lover.

"Mm-hmm."

Laurie ran his hand over James's back. "Want me to fuck you, then?" he asked his boyfriend in turn.

James looked back at him over his shoulder. "Take a wild guess."

"I'll get some lube." Laurie looked at Al. "We're doing things gently, after all. I'm sure you boys can entertain yourselves in my absence."

"We might just manage," Al agreed, tangling his legs around James's.

"You two really do look bloody gorgeous together," Laurie said, standing at the door for a second and watching them, but they were too busy to answer.

By the time Laurie came back, things had moved on. Al's legs were parted, and James was now lying between them, his mouth busy against Al's entrance, licking him open bit by bit. Al groaned, hitching his knees up to his chest to give James better access, and James took full advantage, grazing his teeth gently against the sensitive skin before continuing to kiss and lick Al. Laurie pressed a hand to his cock. It was too fucking hot watching Al squirm under James's ministrations. James's tongue pushed in a little way, penetrating Al, and Al made an indescribable noise, his eyes squeezing shut and his breathing unsteady.

"Fucking hell, James," Laurie murmured, taking up a position behind his boyfriend and slathering lube onto his fingers.

He pressed a slick finger to James's hole, and James mumbled something encouraging, pushing back against him until Laurie slid the finger inside him. Laurie fucked him open slowly as James continued to play with Al's arse with his mouth and tongue. Al was fisting his own cock, now fully hard, and Laurie had rarely seen anything so sexy as his two lovers.

"I need you—to—fuck me," Al gasped out, opening his eyes and giving James a pleading look.

James lifted his head and smiled at Al. "Need to open you a bit more first," he said.

"Allow me." Laurie removed his fingers from James's arse, pushing them gently into Al's.

"God, did you...are you...fucking us both open with the same fingers?"

"Yep," Laurie kissed James's face. "Complaining?"

"Hell no."

"I'd fuck you both, if I could," Laurie said, his voice low and sensual.

"You will be," James said quietly, picking up the lube and squeezing some onto his cock.

Laurie knew what he meant. Behind James, his motions would affect the way James fucked Al, pushing his boyfriend into their lover as he thrust. In that way, he really was fucking them both. James slid himself into Al, just the head of his cock, and Al gave a sigh of relief. Then Laurie was lubing himself up and pushing into James, and the three of them were joined one to the other—deeper, deeper, until Laurie was balls-deep in James and James the same in Al.

"Fuck, that feels good," Al murmured, his hand still busy on his cock. James pushed his hand aside and replaced it with his own, still slippery with lube. "That feels even better," Al added.

Laurie began to move. James, too, their movements separate to begin with before they fell into a pattern. Laurie into James; James forward, driving into Al. Al canting his hips up, encouraging his lovers to more. James smelt of sweat and sex and lube, and Laurie buried his head against James's back, breathing him in, trailing a tongue against the salty damp skin. He heard—felt—the way James's breaths were becoming shallower, faster; could hear Al muttering curse words and encouragement half under his breath as James fucked him and wanked him. James came first, the predictable result of being both giver and receiver simultaneously. His orgasm clenched his arse around Laurie's cock, whilst his hand still continued its motion on Al's.

Al's cries were getting louder: a litany of "Fuck, yes, James, yes, Laurie, fuck..." as he felt James pulse inside him. Laurie just saw the moment when it overtook him, and his cock spurted through James's fingers—the sight was too much, and Laurie came hard, panting against James's spine and feeling his whole body convulse.

How long it lasted, Laurie couldn't have said. It felt both as if it went on forever and as if it were only a second or two before the three of them were lying in a muddled heap on the bed, heavy breathing the only sound in the air. After a while, James reached out a hand and rescued the duvet, pulling it over them. He was still in the middle between Al and Laurie, his head on Al's shoulder, Laurie's body warmly tucked up against his back. Laurie stretched out an arm across James's side, his hand resting possessively on Al's belly, and for a while there was silence and the warm, smug atmosphere of three men who were feeling thoroughly well-fucked. Finally, however, Laurie spoke.

"So you'll stay?" he asked Al, curled up firmly against James's long, lean torso.

"For a bit. Wouldn't want to destroy James's delicate peace of mind, after all," Al said lazily.

James groaned and elbowed Laurie without looking round. "He's never going to let me forget that."

"Like so many other things. You'll get used to it," Laurie said unsympathetically.

Al chuckled sleepily. "Airborne porcine," he murmured.

Laurie's lips twitched. "Shut up, Al."

"I'm going to," Al said, his voice drowsy. He pulled the duvet more thoroughly around himself and snuggled back in against James even more closely than before. "Going to sleep now. Might actually sleep for once, too. And just for the record, I'm pretty damn fond of both of you, too. But as James would say, 'Don't quote me on that'. Night night."

PART 2: AL

4 MONTHS LATER

CHAPTER EIGHT

Al and Laurie sat at opposite ends of the huge sofa, Laurie's pride and joy. Each was focused on their laptop. Laurie was marking a chapter of his first graduate student's PhD, Al working on the script of his latest film. Between them, his head resting on Laurie's lap, his legs flung across Al's, lay James, headphones on, picking songs for his guitar pupils to learn to play. And suddenly, out of nowhere, Al realised he was happy. It was a ridiculous realisation. Al was always happy. He was the most consistently cheerful person in the world. Of course he was happy.

But happy now? Like this? Doing nothing? Working, for fuck's sake! Granted, Al loved film-making; he was, some might say, obsessed by it. And he was pretty sure that the current project, *Transparent*, would be his best yet. But he was doing nothing special now, just blocking in moves, camera angles. The hundred little things which would make filming run more smoothly (only "more" smoothly—nothing ever made filming run smoothly) when they started. The film's title was a play on words; the story was a 'window' into the life of a fourteen-year-old girl, who was honest and open (transparent) about her feelings and emotions as her mother transitioned from a woman to a man—so was, literally, a transgender parent (a trans parent). It was a story of family love, and above all of hope, and it mattered hugely to Al, who was desperate for his own passion—especially given the talent of his lead actor, a transman himself—to bleed through into the film as a whole. Blocking, however, didn't generally engender a sense of great enjoyment in him. Yet with James's calves resting heavily on his thighs, jerking occasionally in time with the music on his headphones; with Laurie sitting almost within touching distance, a little frown of concentration on his face as he waded through the convoluted arguments of his student; Al felt a sudden burst of happiness which lit him from the inside out. Happy. So happy, just sitting here quietly with the people he loved.

Loved?

Al froze. Al didn't do love. Al emphatically did not do love. It was his one main rule. Friendship, definitely. Sex—hell, as much of it as possible. Love, absolutely not. Laurie and James were his best friends.

They were also a devoted couple. Admittedly, they were both his friends *and* a couple with whom he had sex on a fairly regular basis, but there was no more to it than that. Friends with benefits. Al was also having sex with a great number of other people—some regularly, some as a one-off. He wasn't in love with any of them (thank you very much) and had no intention of being so. Ever. Especially not his best friends. Imagine how awkward that could be.

Yes, imagine.

The trouble with having thought it, however, was once thought, it could not be forgotten. It lingered there in Al's mind like a bruise. Occasionally, something would set it off: James would smile at him or Laurie tease him, and Al would twinge with the realisation that the feelings he had for these two men were like nothing he'd ever experienced before. Or he would test it, prodding at his mind like at a sore patch to see if the love-bruise was still there, and discover that it was. Al could tell himself as many times as he liked that he didn't do love, but apparently his mind—his heart?—wasn't listening. One thing he was certain about, however: there was no way on earth he was ever telling James or Laurie how he felt. That would be suicidal.

Everything was made more awkward because of the sheer amount James and Laurie *touched*. Passing gestures usually—a whispered kiss to the neck, fingers trailing across a thigh. But it was by no means unknown for Al to walk into the kitchen to find Laurie on his knees sucking James's cock, James's half-poured coffee temporarily forgotten in front of him. Al was difficult to embarrass and even harder to shock, so he couldn't honestly say that it bothered him—indeed, it was actually very enjoyable to watch two extremely fit men get it on—but for someone who had lived in student housing and then alone, it was a distinct change. And now that he'd realised how he felt about his sometime lovers, it sent a sort of tingling sensation through him, watching them together. He was disconcerted by the way the habit translated to himself, as well. He jolted with surprise when Laurie stroked a possessive hand across his arse as Al was reaching up to get a glass from the cupboard. His reaction triggered one in Laurie, who jerked back as if he had been burnt.

"God, sorry, Al," he said hastily. "I shouldn't do that sort of thing without asking first. That's totally unacceptable."

Al understood the anxiety. As a shameless flirt, he nonetheless was always extremely careful that any touching he did was thoroughly consensual. However, he had anything but an aversion to sexy men touching his bum, most especially if they were Laurie or James. So he turned with a grin, winding an arm around Laurie's neck.

"Nothing to apologise for," he assured him. "Extremely pleasurable. Just unexpected. But please, do continue."

"It's just that Jamie and I...well..." Laurie said apologetically.

Al's grin broadened. "I'd noticed." He pressed his lips to Laurie's. "As long as I'm allowed to respond in kind, I'd positively encourage it."

"Thank god for that," Laurie said. "I didn't want you thinking we'd invited you to live here just so we could molest you in the kitchen."

Al snorted with laughter. "You didn't? How disappointing."

"No," Laurie said, his own smile appearing. "That's just an added bonus." He pulled Al closer into his arms and kissed him with more force.

"Mm, that looks good," commented a new voice. "Can anyone join in?"

James walked over to them, sliding one hand suggestively over Al's body whilst doing the same with the other over Laurie's.

"James," Laurie said reproachfully, "I was just telling Al that we *didn't* invite him here just so we could molest him in the kitchen."

"What, and you were then trying to prove it by...molesting him in the kitchen?" James asked, amused.

"Um, something like that?" Laurie admitted.

"Well," James said suggestively, "why don't we demonstrate it further by molesting him elsewhere? The kitchen's a bit small for an orgy, after all."

"Three isn't an orgy," Al objected, and James winked at him.

"You'd know. Been in many orgies, Al?"

"One," he admitted. It had been all right. Nothing that made him particularly want to repeat the experience, however, though he wouldn't say it wasn't possible. Most things were possible in Al's sex life, and he was open to them all. "Not that I'm objecting to the rest, you understand." He leaned across and pressed his lips to James's, waiting for James's response before opening his mouth and deepening the kiss.

"Apparently not," James said, after a little pause whilst they both savoured the moment. "Well, bedroom, anyone?"

"If we have to," Laurie said, deliberately unconvincing.

"Apparently we have to," Al told him. "Jamie says, and as you know, what Jamie says goes."

"I know that for sure," Laurie agreed.

James laughed. "It's a sad life for both of you," he said unsympathetically. "Now, come and be ravished, the pair of you."

In the bedroom, the three of them undressed each other, piece by piece—James's hands on Al's shirt as Al tugged at Laurie's belt; Laurie then removing James's trousers with the ease of someone who had done it so many times before. When they were all naked, James pulled Al against his body so that they were pressed up close. Laurie stood behind Al again, flush against his skin, his cock pushing down into the cleft of Al's arse. Al never really thought of himself as short—at just over five foot eight, he was of moderate height—but squeezed between his lovers' bodies like this, he suddenly felt an overwhelming awareness of their size. And there was something very hot about being sandwiched between two much bigger men, Al thought, as Laurie and James kissed across his shoulder. For both of his lovers were over six foot, and broader than slender Al as well. He was surrounded by their bodies, and fuck but it felt good, especially with Laurie grinding against his arse and James moving his hips in little suggestive circles into his front. Al sucked on James's neck, making him groan into Laurie's mouth, and pressed his hands into the small of James's back.

"God," said Laurie at last, finally pulling away from James's kiss and rubbing himself up against Al with more purpose, "you've got such a shaggable arse, Al."

Al smiled into James's shoulder. "Intending to demonstrate?" he asked.

"With your permission," Laurie said promptly.

Al rocked back against him, his hands dropping to fondle James's bum as he pretended to consider the matter. "I think that might be acceptable."

"Mm-hmm?" Laurie dropped a kiss on the top of Al's head. "Well, then, unless you want me to fuck you up against James—an idea which certainly has its merits—can I suggest you come to bed?"

"You can," Al agreed. He looked up at James and gave in to the desire to kiss him. James did not seem to object. "And you, James?" he asked afterwards. "Anything you're intending to do? Just out of a matter of interest, you know."

"I'm going to fuck you after Laurie's just had you," James said, hot dark eyes on him. "I want to fuck my boyfriend's lover when it's so bloody clear you've just been with him. Okay?"

Al laughed. "Like I'm going to say no. 'Oh no, Jamie, don't fuck me. You know how I hate it,'" he mocked. "God, that sounds hot."

"You're so filthy, the pair of you," Laurie said. He was pulling Al towards the bed as the other two flirted. "And no, that's not a complaint."

Al slid casually onto the bed, hands touching any part of Laurie he could reach as Laurie leaned over to grab lube from the bedside table. James strolled over and joined in with wandering hands, sitting down beside the pair and apparently having no preference as to whether his hands were on his boyfriend or his sometime lover. Al sighed, stretching eagerly under the touch when James's hands were on him, and James laughed.

"Thought it was Laurie you were wanting just now?"

"I do," Al assured him. "*And* you." He made a soft, contented noise. "As you bloody well know."

"Sure you don't just want James?" Laurie asked, his finger circling Al's hole, lubing him up as he spoke.

"Quite sure. When are you going to fuck me?" Al asked. He hitched his hips up against Laurie's finger so that it breached the ring of muscle. "I want you, Laurie. I want you inside me."

"Demanding little slut." Laurie's face was amused, though.

"But can I suck you, James, as he fucks me? Please, god, please." Al wanted all of his lovers he could get, in every possible way. He wasn't above begging for it if necessary.

"Insatiable," Laurie murmured.

James had his gorgeous lopsided smile on. Al had known him for years, but that expression still turned him on like nothing else. "No need to call me 'god', Al love. I expect I might deign to allow you to suck me off. Just for your sake, obviously."

Al groaned luxuriously. Tried not to think about the 'love' that James had so casually added to his name. James had never done that before. "Fuck. Want you both so much. Please."

"On all fours then, so I can watch James as you have your mouth around his cock," Laurie instructed.

Al wriggled round, pressing kisses to the insides of James's thighs, concentrating his attention on James. He knew that Laurie's adoration of James was such that one of the best ways to turn Laurie on was to get James hard and wanting—plus, of course, Al adored sucking cock to an almost embarrassing degree. He licked a stripe up the underside of James's cock, just as Laurie ran three fingers across his arse, pushing the middle one inside him.

"God," Al said involuntarily, pressing back against Laurie and simultaneously swirling his tongue around the head of James's cock.

"So open, Al," Laurie said. "So many men, so little time? You're so ready for me, aren't you?"

"Mmm."

Al did not tell him that with all the sex he got here with Laurie and James, he usually fucked other men rather than getting them to fuck him. That was his one regret about his lovers—Laurie would never bottom, and James was monogamous to Laurie in that one regard. Al loved (loved loved) being fucked, but that didn't mean he never wanted to fuck someone else. If he was open and ready for Laurie, it was because of Laurie and James's previous actions. And they were both going to fuck him today. He closed his eyes to savour that thought, feeling Laurie press his cock up against him.

But Laurie was a tease and just left him waiting; it seemed he wanted Al to continue with sucking off James before taking things any further. Al could feel his lover just *there* at his entrance. He wanted him inside so damn badly, but Laurie just laughed and rocked back with him when Al tried to thrust back against his cock.

"Bastard," Al mumbled around James's cock, turning his attention back to that instead.

He'd been right about Laurie's intentions—as soon as James was beginning to pant a little, Laurie pushed inside him, making Al groan wholeheartedly around James's cock. Fuck, it felt so good to be filled at both ends. There was nothing like it, the knowledge that two men were taking their pleasure from you. Giving it to you. He sucked harder as Laurie began to fuck him, starting with long, slow thrusts which sent shivers through Al. James's breathing was getting faster; when Al looked up through his eyelashes at him, he could see the expression on James's face, which showed he was getting close. James looked down at him and grinned ruefully, pushing Al away.

"'F I want to fuck you, you're going to have to stop that," he said regretfully. A smile slid over his face as he lifted his eyes to watch Laurie taking Al a little quicker now. "And I want to fuck you. Right after Laurie has. But I'm going to make you come first."

James moved position so that he could reach under Al and slide his hand around Al's cock. It was almost all Al needed to come, after having had the taste of James's pre-come in his mouth, the continuing sensation of Laurie fucking up against his prostate and filling him so damn full.

"Fuck, yes, that," Al said breathlessly as James began to move his hand.

"Yeah?" James leaned over and kissed Al's open mouth, running his tongue around Al's lips.

Al moaned. And moaned again as Laurie upped the pace once more, and James kept time with him, wanking Al faster and faster.

"Oh god, please, yes, please," Al begged, shoving back against Laurie and forward into James's hand over and over, lost in the tempo, barely aware of what he was saying. "Yes. Oh fuck, please."

"So hot," James murmured, and that was the final spur.

Al came, moaning shamelessly as he did so, aware that behind him Laurie was thrusting so damn hard that he might just split apart on Laurie's cock—and that he might just love it as he did so, too. Laurie came quietly, the diametric opposite to Al, and Al could feel James's gaze switching between the pair of them, his cheeks flushed with arousal as he watched them both ride out their orgasms.

"So. Fucking. Hot," James repeated.

Laurie pulled out of Al and moved to kiss James. Al collapsed onto his front on the bed, his heart racing, his limbs all relaxed. James had given himself up to kissing Laurie with the enthusiasm he always gave to that. Al just watched them until James looked up.

"Roll over, Al. I want you on your back."

Because of course, they weren't finished now. Al's stomach was sticky with come, and he could feel Laurie's seed filling his arse. He rolled over, and James started stroking himself. He was mostly hard already, but he slid his fingers through what was left of Al's come and wet his cock with that.

"You going to fuck me now, Jamie?" Al asked.

James hitched him a smile. "Mm-hmm. Like you wouldn't beg me to if I said no."

"I'll beg if you want," Al said, tilting his hips and spreading his legs for his other lover.

"So shameless," Laurie commented, sliding down so that he was lying beside Al, both of them looking at up James.

"Beg me then," James said.

Al flicked him a glance. Didn't bother pretending to object. Instead, he said at once, "I want you inside me. Please, James. Please fuck me. You know I want you."

"Spread your legs further for me. Open yourself up for me."

Al did so. "Please, Jamie," he said again.

"God. You look good," James said, entering him in one fluid movement, sliding inside Al's wet, slick arse.

It felt amazing. So wet. So fucking sexy, knowing that James was sliding through Laurie's come. Knowing that he'd been fucked well once, and he was about to be fucked well for a second time. God, Al would do anything to feel like this. Laurie, beside Al, lay lazy and satisfied. His hand went up to stroke James's face, and his voice, when he spoke, was warm and sensual.

"God, James," he said, his eyes lingering on him, "fucking Al's used hole like that. Wanting your cock covered in someone else's come. You're so dirty, so fucking filthy, Jamie." The way he said it made his words an endearment.

James, his eyes meeting Laurie's with blazing heat, nonetheless said nothing. He started to thrust inside Al instead, jerking his hips back and forth in a steady motion.

Al couldn't help himself, lying back and moaning "James" at the feeling.

Laurie turned his attention to Al at that, dropping his hand from James to run it over Al's chest. Laurie had such large hands. Al had always loved Laurie's hands. Especially when they were touching him like this.

"As for you, gorgeous Al," Laurie murmured, kissing the side of his face, "you've already come, too, and you should be too sensitive for anything after I fucked you, but instead of acting like it, you're lying here with James inside you. Lying here on *my* bed at *my* side, moaning out *my* boyfriend's name. God, you're such a slut." His hand stroked lower. "Half hard again, as well. Is Jamie doing you well, Al? Hitting your prostate over and over, making you see stars? Making you want to beg for him some more?"

"Oh, bloody fuck," James hissed; and Al, looking up at him, could see that Laurie's words were turning him on further.

Al couldn't blame him—Laurie was outrageously sexy when he started talking dirty. Al suspected it was his slow, deep-toned voice in combination with the things he chose to say. He knew his partners well, knew what got them off, and loved to give it to them. James was pumping his hips harder now, thrusting into Al over and over, Laurie's comments about Al's prostate truer than ever. Al was moaning steadily again, never good at keeping quiet about his pleasure, and Laurie was stroking his cock over and over until he was fully hard again and wanting.

"So fucking sexy, you two," Laurie whispered, his mouth a little open as his breathing faltered, watching James take Al hard and fast.

"Please, James—Laurie," Al whined, not sure who to plead with. James inside him and Laurie's hand on his cock. He shifted underneath James, one leg pulled back, the other wrapped around his best friend and lover.

"God, yes," panted James.

It took only a few more thrusts before he was coming, filling Al's arse so full of come that it dribbled out of the edges, running down his thighs and the crack between his buttocks. Al knew he must look totally wrecked, covered in come; completely the slut Laurie called him, and he didn't care because he was *so close* to coming again. Just a little bit more—a little—he squeezed his eyes shut, and then Laurie did something with his hand on Al's cock which was just perfect. Al cried out. His orgasm was briefer this time, but intense; white hot spikes of electricity seeming to shiver through him.

When it was over, they lay there together, silent, sticky and satisfied. Al hadn't used to like cuddling; once the main event was over, it was over. Time to get on with the next thing—for Al always had a mind for the next new adventure, not necessarily sex-related. But over the past four months particularly, whilst he'd been living with Laurie and James, he'd become converted. James and Laurie were always at it, whether presex, post-coital, or entirely separate from any sexual activity; and Al had discovered that there was a warmth and sensuality about being wrapped in someone else's arms (or two someone elses' arms) that had a different sort of pleasure attached to it. The others had been tactful enough not to comment on his change of attitude, instead, just reaching out for him with the same willingness they showed for each other. Al loved it.

"Well," he said lazily at last, "feel free to molest me in the kitchen at any time if it leads to this."

Laurie laughed. "I won't dare touch you now unless James is in the house, just in case it does," he said, referring to the usually unspoken agreement that Al had sex with James and Laurie as a couple but not with merely one or the other.

"Al knows all about that," James said confidently, and Al felt his heart warm at James's unswerving trust in him. James was right, of course—Al would never break his trust. But it felt good to hear it stated so clearly.

Al smiled. "Okay..." he relented, "okay, you've got me. Feel free to molest me in the kitchen at any time anyway. Even if it doesn't."

Laurie leaned across and kissed him, his eyes amused. "Now that," he said, "sounds more like our Al."

"Meantime," Al said, suddenly realising the time, "I'm supposed to be at the wine shop in just over half an hour, and probably Fen would prefer it if I was dressed and not quite so covered in your spunk." He rolled himself regretfully up and out of bed. "Bugger it, who works on a Sunday?"

CHAPTER NINE

But if Laurie and James were Al's housemates and most regular lovers, they were certainly not his only ones—nor were they his only long-term partners. Al had been meeting up with Gemma Braeburn for no-strings sex for years now, though he hadn't seen her in months, thanks to her work having taken her abroad. This was a common thing for her. Al knew that one of the things she liked about him was the fact that he wasn't bothered by her absence and was happy to pick up where they'd left off as soon as she was back in the country. He appreciated her casualness equally. Plus, she was an excellent person and a great deal of fun to be with, which meant, all in all, Al and Gemma had an extremely good time both in and out of bed. When she'd texted him the previous day asking when he was free, he'd been speedy in his response to her and was now waiting patiently at the clock tower where they'd agreed to meet. True to his usual habit, he was five minutes early, and he leaned back against the cold stone, enjoying the warmth of the summer evening as he waited.

He didn't need to wait long; Gemma was precisely on time.

"Gemma!" Al couldn't contain his delight at seeing her again, and she flung her arms around him with equal enthusiasm.

"Hey, stranger. Long time, no see."

He rolled his eyes, slinging an arm around her companionably as they pulled apart. "Well, if you will be foolish enough to jet off to far-flung places without me... How was it, by the way? And how long have you been home?"

"Good. Knackering, but good." Gemma pushed her hair back from her face. She looked gorgeous, as always, but Al could see she was tired. She was a backing singer with a well-known band, just back after a little over four months touring the US. "Twenty different states. Don't ask me where we've been—I lost any ability to keep up about three weeks in. As to how long I've been home—four days." She smiled at him. "Thought I'd catch up with my favourite guy."

Al laughed at that. "Gem, dear, you flatter me." Though, to be fair, she was his closest female friend. He wondered if he could talk to her about Laurie and James... No. Some things weren't for sharing. "So, what do you fancy doing now?"

"What are the options?" Gemma put her arm around him in return, and they started walking, though neither of them knew where they were going. They were much of a height; Gemma was just over an inch shorter than Al, at five foot seven, but in her heels the difference was minimised. "No, let me guess—food or sex."

"We-ell, if that's what you want," Al retorted, grinning. "We could go bowling if you really wanted."

"Al darling, I never want to go bowling," Gemma assured him. "Food first. Then sex. How does that sound?"

"Like my sort of evening," Al said.

☆☆☆

They went to a Chinese restaurant they both knew well. The food was sublime, but it was little known by the wider world, so they had some degree of privacy (always important, as Gemma was apt to be photographed if she ventured anywhere popular)—plus the prices were not as extortionate as in many parts of London. *That* was important for Al, who was by no means rich. Gemma kept Al laughing with her tales of her on-and-offstage exploits; like Al himself, she was a fascinating storyteller, with a self-deprecating sense of humour. Confusions between US and UK language and culture ("trust me, Al, when someone apologised for touching my fanny unintentionally, I nearly died"), the all-out fight which nearly erupted between two of her band mates over whose turn it was to ring for room service, and the occasion on which she fell "arse-over-tit on stage" were all dragged out and made into hilarious anecdotes. At the same time, she let him into a bit of the more emotional stuff—her feelings being so long from England ("I missed my parents...and bourbon biscuits. God, how I missed bourbons!") and her fear when she had a cold that the singer the band hired to replace her temporarily would make them realise that she wasn't up to the job.

In return, Al regaled her with stories of his own life. The new film he was currently putting together and his hopes that it could even surpass his last one, *Welding the Night Away*. Half embarrassed of his minor success compared to Gemma's fame, he neglected to mention the fact that *Welding* had been nominated for several awards—something she twitted him on, having read it on the Internet.

"I gather the last one bombed," she said with a serious face.

Al dug into the last of his noodles. "Oh, it wasn't as bad as that," he said.

She kicked him under the table. "I know, idiot. I do actually get to look at the Internet, even in America. I saw the reviews—and the award nominations. Were you thinking of telling me anything about it?"

"Ah." Al was embarrassed, and he knew he looked it. "Well," he said, recovering his composure with his usual speed, "I did consider spending the evening telling you how bloody talented I was, but I presumed you already knew. I'm happy to do it for the rest of the night if you want, however." He looked up at her innocently.

Gemma pulled a considering face. "Nice though the offer is, I have some other things I can think of that we could be doing. Have you finished yet?" Al spooned the last mouthful of his meal into his mouth and nodded. "Okay, then. Your place or mine?"

"Whichever's easiest for you," Al said easily. "If yours is all over bags or whatever you jet setters bring back from all over the world, come to mine, but if you feel like you've barely seen your house—or," he added with a grin, "you want to re-christen it, if you've not done so already with someone else—that's good with me too. I've moved, by the way—I think I mentioned it? I'm living with Laurie and James at the moment, but that makes no difference. They won't disturb us. Probably too busy shagging each other, anyway."

"Please, can we have the bill?" Gemma asked the waiter politely. She turned back to Al. "You said you'd moved—but living with other people? You? Seriously?"

"Yeah, well," said Al uncomfortably, aware of the depths within depths behind his current living arrangements into which he didn't particularly want to delve. The fact that he'd been assaulted didn't seem like a particularly jolly conversation for Gemma's first night back with him. "Seemed a good idea at the time. They're not exactly high maintenance, and Jamie's a bloody amazing cook."

Gemma giggled. "If I ever want a character reference, remind me not to come to you. 'Not high maintenance and one of 'em can cook.' Charming." They split the bill, and she took his hand as they got up. "Let's go to mine. It's closer, anyway. And I'm sure you can step over the bags."

"I expect I could manage," Al assured her seriously, and hand in hand, they walked back to Gemma's flat.

Her home was in a smarter part of town and more impressive than anywhere Al had lived. But it didn't bother either of them—that had been the case since their earliest dates, one of the side effects of sleeping with a celebrity. Gemma knew that Al was not swayed either way by her fame; she liked it, in fact. So Al, as usual, walked in as if he owned the place, looking round appreciatively but otherwise saying nothing. Gemma had been joking about the bags; the place was pristine.

"Come to bed," Gemma invited, kissing him.

"Thought you'd never ask," teased Al. They went into the bedroom, and he flung himself across Gemma's luxurious bed, rumpling the neat, previously uncreased covers. "So, what's on this menu tonight? Hope it's as good as the food."

Gemma looked at him from across the room. "What do you say to my fucking you?" she questioned, raising her eyebrows. "I had plenty of blokes to have sex with in the usual manners when I was away, but quite apart from the fact that there was no way I was taking a strap-on through American Customs, there's precious few men who are into that sort of thing. And fewer still I can ask about it."

"In other words, Gemma darling," Al drawled, his expression teasing, "you couldn't find anyone who lives up to me in the whole of the States."

She grinned. "You can put it that way if you like, Al. I should've known you would, to be fair. So, fancy getting fucked tonight?"

The drawl stayed. The teasing expression, however, moved to a hotter, more sensual one. "I'm always up for getting fucked," Al said. "You know that."

She blew him a kiss. "Is there anything you're not up for, darling?"

"When it comes to you? Unlikely."

Al liked sex. He liked all sorts of sex. Specifically, he liked sex with Gemma a great deal. She was good in bed—imaginative, lively and generous. As she stripped, he admired her beautiful feminine body; so very different from the men he slept with. James had once asked him, if he had to sleep with just men or just women for the rest of his life, which Al would choose. Al had been unable to answer; he loved the differences. Each man and each woman was different, but the variance between a woman's soft breasts and wet pussy and a man's firm chest and hard cock was so great. He drank her in with his eyes and then welcomed her to her own bed with all the sensuality inherent in his own nature.

Afterwards, they lay together under her duvet, chatting idly. Al always enjoyed Gemma in her post-coital state: relaxed, happy and slightly off-kilter. No longer quite as extroverted, wanting to talk non-stop. He supposed the same might be said for him, and was amused by the comparison.

"There's a reason I come back to you," Gemma said.

"I know." Al smiled.

She shoved him. "Not that!"

Al shook his head. "See, people always misunderstand me." He met Gemma's eyes. "It's terribly sad, you know. I didn't mean what you thought I meant." He had kept his tone light up until this point, waiting to discover what he saw in Gemma's face. What he saw made him continue, his voice suddenly serious. "You see me as an actual person," he said carefully.

She blinked, surprised. "Yes."

"Most people don't." He stretched languidly. "Which is not a problem. Don't get me wrong, I enjoy having sex with plenty of people. But I don't necessarily come back, any more than you do."

The intelligence that was part of the reason he liked her so much shone clearly in her eyes as she looked at him. "Yes," she said slowly. "I see. I'm not wrong, then, to think we're friends."

Al laughed out loud at that, leaning up to kiss her. "Oh, Gem! No, you're not wrong."

"You barely contact me while I'm away."

"Excuse me," Al pointed out, "you don't exactly fling yourself my way, either."

"Fair point," she admitted.

"You're one of my best friends, you know," Al said. "And no, I don't have masses."

"You're one of mine, too," Gemma said. Then she added, "What, you mean apart from the pair you live with?"

"Mmm," said Al, thinking about James and Laurie and his problem. Then, in a burst of confidence he was certain he would later regret, "God, Gem, can I tell you something?" He hesitated. "I haven't told anyone about this, okay?"

"Okay." Gemma rolled over to face him, looking worried. "What's happened? You okay?"

"I did something terrible when you were away," Al said in a voice of doom.

Gemma sat up in bed, dragging the duvet around her. "What do you mean? Al, seriously—you're not teasing me?"

"No." Al turned over and buried his face in the covers. "God, I don't know what to do."

"Tell me," she ordered.

"Ifellinlove," he mumbled into the pillow.

"Huh?" She leaned over and dragged his mouth free, tugging him round so that she could see his face. "Now try that again audibly."

"I fell in love," Al said miserably, his eyes shut so he couldn't see her.

There was utter silence. A silence which felt more meaningful—uncomfortably so—than any Al had ever known in his dealings with Gemma. He opened an eye cautiously to look at her, to see if he could gauge what she was thinking.

"What?" she said at last.

"You heard," he said, shutting his eye again quickly.

Another pause. "Are you trying to let me down gently or something, Al?" she asked slowly. "Was tonight a kind of last hurrah? The friendship comment a hint that you just want to be friends?"

Al turned over and opened both eyes at that. "What? No! Bloody hell, no. Why would you think that?"

"Well, if you're in love... I mean, seriously?"

"Yes."

"Sorry," she apologised. "I had to check. It sounds so unlikely coming from your mouth."

"Tell me about it," he said ruefully, leaning over and resting his head on her leg.

"But—doesn't that mean you're doing the whole commitment and fidelity and whatever stuff? Who is it? Male or female? Or neither, given it's you," she added, having had one of Al's lectures in the past on the possibility of being non-binary or genderqueer.

"You can't be in a band and still not know anyone who's non-binary," Al objected, avoiding the main issue neatly. "And fuck me; I have no intention of doing monogamy. Anyone who knows me knows that. Geez." He winced.

"Actually, it turns out I *can* be in a band without that," Gemma said dryly. "Plus, I already did fuck you. And, by the way, you're not answering the question. Who?"

"James and Laurie," Al confessed.

"Your flatmates?" Then Gemma took in what he had said and blinked slowly. "Hang on...James *and* Laurie?" Al nodded. "Both of them?"

Al nodded again. "Apparently so." He hesitated. "Thing is, they don't know. And I'm not telling them. And...and..." He hated himself for how pathetic he sounded, but he'd had no one to talk to about this, no one at all. Usually he talked to James about everything; this was the one time in his life where that wasn't an option, and it had thrown him for a loop. "What am I going to do about it, Gem?" he begged.

"Is it that awful?"

"It's a disaster! I'm so humiliated!"

Gemma had been looking amused, but there was clearly something in Al's face to show that he genuinely did feel this way about it, for her mood sobered. "What's the problem?" she asked.

"Well, for a start, I can't tell them about it," Al said. "They're a couple, for god's sake. You know, a proper couple. And I'm just...me. Plus they're my best friends, and if I mention anything about this, it'll make it all weird, and I don't do weird. I just don't."

"Al, love, you do weird better than anyone I've ever met," Gemma put in, gently teasing. "But I get your point."

"I do *weird* weird. I don't do 'falling in love' weird. Fucking hell, Gem, James was in love with Laurie for six years before they got together. It was awful. I knew I was never going there, ever."

"I'm not sure it's something you get a choice about," Gemma commented. "Can't you tell them?"

"Hell no! I told you—weird. And it's, like, affecting other stuff. I told you we were sharing a house, right? I keep not wanting to go out, just stay in and hang with them. And they probably want me out of there so they can do couple-y things—whatever it is that couples do. Fuck knows I was never any good at that, even when I tried dating."

"Apart from the sex, you mean?"

"Apart from that," Al agreed. "I was good at that bit." He looked up at her from his position on her lap. "Still am," he added smugly.

She batted his head. "Some things haven't changed then. You're still as big-headed as ever."

"Still want to have sex with you, too," Al assured her. "And other people. Just—not as much." He grinned up at her. "You, as much sex as you want. But...I can't quite be arsed going out and meeting people all the time, you know? If someone turns up, and we get on; that's all well and good. But…why go out and make the effort if you can just stay in and be happy that way? Bloody hell, it just sounds wrong when you say it out loud, doesn't it?"

"It sounds flipping odd coming from you," Gemma admitted. "But not 'wrong'." She stroked his head thoughtfully, as if he were a cat. Al had often thought that he'd rather like to be a cat. "What do you like about them? I mean, don't get me wrong, I've met them both, and they seem like nice blokes, but there's got to be a bit more to it than that."

Al sighed. "I'm going to sound like an idiot. I know I am. It's just, Laurie–"

"He's the bigger one with light brown hair, yes?" asked Gemma.

"Yeah. Big." Al sighed again, but this time it had a dreamy note in it. "Big, strong hands. He's got these gorgeous big hands, but at the same time he's so gentle…"

"Hold on a minute," said Gemma, frowning. "Wasn't he the one who painted your arse a lovely shade of red shortly before I went away?"

Al found a reminiscent smile on his face at this reminder. He had deliberately wound Laurie up to see what effect it would have, and Laurie had delivered an extremely satisfying spanking–followed by an equally satisfying fucking. It had been glorious. When Al had met up with Gemma a couple of days later, the marks had still been clearly visible. Evidently, it had been a memorable occasion for more than just him.

"Mmm," he said happily. He shook himself, bringing himself back to the present moment. "Well, that doesn't mean he can't give it out when he wants to," he added. "But I like that, too. He's laid-back most of the time, though. Kind, thoughtful. Someone you can rely upon, you know? Still, he can be very dominating when he wants to."

"Apparently so," Gemma said.

"He just kind of makes me feel…owned," Al admitted.

Gemma looked at Al with something approaching surprise. "I wouldn't have thought that was your sort of thing," she commented.

"Says the girl who just fucked me," Al pointed out. He shrugged, blushing a bit. "You're right, though. Please don't tell anyone I said that, especially not Laurie. I'd be mortified."

"As if I would." Gemma leaned over and shrugged on a baby doll negligee. "Anyway, you've got much more over me than the other way around. 'The Girl Who Fucked Me. Sassy Strap-ons Do It For Backing

Singer Gemma Braeburn Of Popular Band' et cetera, et cetera... The press would love it. But you wouldn't do it to me. And you know me better than to think I'd let you down."

"I do."

She nodded. "What about James, though? You've said a lot about Laurie, but James? Not so much."

"I couldn't live without James," Al said simply. He saw the flabbergasted expression on Gemma's face and went on. "Oh, I could live without having sex with him, if I had to. I did, for a while, when he and Laurie first got together. About a year, in fact. Bloody weird—we'd been sleeping together for ages before then—but it was fine. It was okay, anyway. Unproblematic. I wasn't pining after him or anything. Good when we started up again, but it was not the end of the world when we weren't. It's in a different way I need James. He's not just my best mate; he's my other self. Can't manage without him."

"I see." Gemma's eyes were soft. She reached out and stroked Al's face. "That's really rather sweet."

Al rolled his eyes. "Oh, for god's sake, not sweet. Save me from sweet. The last thing I ever want to be is sweet." He ran a hand through his hair. "See? This is what I've come to. I told you it was a disaster. I said it was awful. I've come to the point where I'm bloody *sweet*."

Gemma dissolved into giggles at his rant. "Sorry, darling—didn't mean to offend."

"It's just so demoralising," Al complained. "I was quite happy as I was, thank you, and suddenly I turn round and damn it all if I haven't gone and fallen in love with my best friends. Next thing I know, I'll be buying a bread maker and talking about pensions and becoming conventional."

Gemma was still giggling. "I think you're safe from that one, hon. You're in love with two guys at once and have every intention of sleeping with various other people as well. I don't think people are going to take one look and go 'oh, that Al Hitchins—so damn conventional!'"

"Maybe not." Al looked over at her. "I guess," he said, embarrassed, "if they actually wanted me to, I'd give monogamy...duogamy, whatever it would be...a go for them. It'd be a disaster waiting to happen—but I'd probably try if they asked. Thing is, they're not interested anyway, and James at least knows me better than that." He groaned. "Still. You don't know any ways of falling out of love with people, do you? If they wouldn't go around being so damn gorgeous, and...and nice, and funny and..."

"You really have got it bad, haven't you?" Gemma put in.

He glared at her. "It's not funny."

"It kind of is," she said, half apologetically, and he gave a reluctant grin.

"Well, I suppose so. For other people, anyway. Me, of all people! This love crap. Bloody hell. And I've had no one to talk to it about either. I talk to Jamie about everything, but this doesn't exactly come into the category of things we can chat through, you know?"

"Well, you've got me. I'm back for a while—we've got a month or so and then only a UK tour." Gemma looked down at him. "I've got to say, I'm dying to meet your blokes again now, though. See the people who can make Al Hitchins fall in love."

"You'd better not say anything to them," Al said hastily.

She rolled her eyes. "Al! As if. But you can't blame me for being curious. And...well..." She raised his hand to her lips and kissed it. "If you need to talk to someone, darling, I'm here. No judgement, I promise—and not even that much teasing." She smiled. "Can't promise none, but—"

"Yeah, well, if things were different, nor could I," Al admitted resignedly. "You're a good mate. Thanks. I just feel so—stupid. Like there's nothing I can do about it except pretend it's not happening, and it's doing my head in. Sorry. Sorry, I didn't mean to unload all of this onto you, especially not when you're only just back off tour."

"I'm flattered," Gemma said. "Now, fancy a glass of champagne? Celebrate my return to home climes, and drown your sorrows at the same time?"

"Sounds good to me."

CHAPTER TEN

Of course Al being Al, being in love didn't mean that he was going to stop teasing Laurie or James any time soon. Even had the circumstances been different, he wasn't one for sweet words and romantic gestures. James was too used to him to get wound up by Al's taunts; instead, Al would find himself with his arm twisted behind his back and a wet cloth thrust down his neck or be informed that the dessert James had made would sadly only feed two hungry men, neither of which happened to be Al. It didn't prevent Al continuing to provoke his best friend of course—this way of interacting had been theirs for fifteen years, and they were hardly going to stop now. But it did mean that Laurie was a more interesting case for study, since although Al had been teasing him for years too, the style and specifics of his incitements had perforce been somewhat different when it was a relationship between a teenager and an older family friend than it could be now that the men were living together—and having sex together not infrequently. Laurie, indeed, had always borne Al's taunting with irritating good humour when they'd been younger. It was fascinating to discover that the closer they became, the more easily Al could find the right buttons to press to have an entirely different effect. As to the right buttons for what precisely...well, that was another matter entirely. Winding up Laurie could be an extremely rewarding pastime if Al judged it right.

Which was why on one particular evening, Al was pursuing a specific line of provocation. Laurie had spent the early part of the night working on some lecture notes for the following academic year and had shut his laptop and leaned back with a sigh.

"Remind me again why I thought becoming a lecturer would be a good plan?" he asked rhetorically.

Ignoring the rhetorical nature of the question, Al responded. "Because you wanted a chance to order young, impressionable teenagers around, obviously," he said, glancing sideways at Laurie.

James gave Al a thoughtful glance over the top of the book he was reading but otherwise showed no sign of having heard him. Laurie, however, turned to him in outrage.

"What did you just say?"

"We-ell," Al articulated further, "you're basically a bit bossy, aren't you? Like to be in charge. Things along those lines."

"Wha—?"

Al didn't even give him a chance to finish his question. "Dominate people a bit," he added. "Something like that?"

"You little..." Laurie stopped, apparently lost for words.

"What," murmured Al softly, "you mean you don't like to get people to do what they're told? Boss around some innocent students like I used to be?" He flicked a glance at Laurie with a mischievous smile. "Tell me you didn't want to order me to behave when you had me in the odd lecture you took."

"It wasn't *then* I wanted you to behave yourself," Laurie said grimly.

"No?" Al reined in the smile a little, but he was bubbling over with amusement and not a little excitement. This was working better even than he had hoped. "Why, whenever was it, Laurie? Because you know you've wanted to, haven't you?"

"It would serve you right if I ordered you to the floor right now and made you do everything I told you," Laurie threatened, getting to his feet and striding over to Al so that he was standing, looking down at the younger man as he sprawled lazily in a chair. "Dominated you so much you didn't even know your own name by the time I'd finished with you."

Al felt his cock hardening even at the thought. His heart gave an extra-strong thump. "Go on then," he challenged, meeting Laurie's gaze square on.

Laurie had an almost feral look in his eyes. For a moment, Al thought (hoped, prayed) he was actually going to take him up on the offer. However, after a pause, he said carefully, "Of course I won't." He glanced away from Al.

"I wouldn't mind."

James had set aside the book and was watching the two of them, his dark eyes flicking between them. He looked interested and not at all unwilling to see it play out to the end.

Laurie caught his breath. "Don't be ridiculous. I'm not—"

"You could be," Al suggested.

"Don't tempt me."

But Al wanted Laurie tempted. God, how he wanted him tempted. He was running out of persuasion, though, so he did what he'd been doing most of his life when he needed a bit of support.

"Jamie," Al said pleadingly to his best friend.

He couldn't let this chance get away from him. The thought of Laurie being explicitly and unrelentingly dominating was turning him on so fucking much. And James always knew what Al was thinking. He'd understand—Al hoped. As always, James didn't let him down. Standing up as well, he slid an arm around Laurie's waist.

"He wants it. In fact, I suspect it's what he's been angling for," he murmured to his boyfriend. He gazed down at Al, taking in the way Al's trousers were tenting round a less-than-subtle erection, and his mouth curled up in a smile. "He wants it very much, I'd say."

"Oh god," said Laurie, his voice unexpectedly husky. He leaned down to where Al was sitting and put a hand under Al's chin, forcing his head up so that their eyes met. There was a question there, and Al met the gaze honestly. Laurie clearly read the message Al was offering. "Bedroom. Then get on your knees," he said, letting go.

Al slipped from the chair and walked through into James and Laurie's room, where he dropped to his knees immediately with a little sigh of relief and gratitude. The other two had followed him, and he could feel their gaze on him. James leaned forward and stroked his hair gently.

"Good boy," he said. Then, with a wry smile, added, "In a manipulative sort of way, that is."

Al looked down at the floor, unable to deny James's veiled accusation. It was all too true. But it had, after all, got him precisely what he was looking for.

"You're going to do what I say, Al," Laurie said.

"Yes."

"Everything I say."

"Yes," Al whispered plaintively.

"Because you want to."

"Yes."

"Yes, Laurie."

"Yes, Laurie."

Al felt his breathing catch and stutter in his chest. Laurie was going to do this for him. Actually going to do it.

"Take James's trousers and pants off," Laurie commanded. "No, don't get up." He looked at James. "All right, James?"

James nodded. "I think I'm capable of telling you if it isn't," he said casually.

"Mm." Laurie's tone was thoughtful. Al had turned to James and was reaching for the button on his jeans. "If it's too much, or there's something you don't want to do, Alistair," he said quietly, "just say your name and we'll stop, all right?"

"Yes, Sir," Al said, unthinkingly.

There was an electric silence, but from the expression on Laurie's face, he hadn't minded the word. Hadn't minded at all, in fact. His blue eyes were darker, pupils wider than Al had ever seen them.

"Good," Laurie said, at length. "Carry on."

Al obediently undid James's trousers and slid his lover out of them with some care.

"I could get used to this," James said with a little smile.

"Make him hard, Al," Laurie said. Al leaned forward to take James's cock between his lips, but Laurie stopped him with a gesture. "No. With your hands. I know how you love a cock in your mouth, Al, but you need to learn other things. You're too mouthy all round, you know. You talk too much. You were an insolent brat in my seminars, and you're still one now, and you need to learn some manners. So you're going to remain totally silent unless given permission to speak or make a noise, understand?"

"Yes, Sir."

Al's cock was throbbing hard against his jeans. From his position on his knees at the other men's feet, his face was level with their groins. His eyes were fixed on James's long, beautiful erection as he worked it between his fingers, but he was constantly aware of the scent of Laurie's arousal, and it was driving him mad. The thought that Laurie wanted to do this to him as much as Al wanted it done. Al wanted to rub his face against Laurie's crotch, breathe him in. He bit back a moan, and suddenly realised how difficult this 'silence' business was going to be. Al was anything but a quiet lover. Not speaking would have been hard enough, but making no noise at all? He had a sudden quiver of anxiety. He knew Laurie wouldn't mind, not really, if he didn't manage it, but he wanted to do it. He wanted to get this right. James had already hardened in his hands, and Al could see his friend's chest rising and falling more swiftly as if his breathing had changed.

"Well done," Laurie said. "Now, put your hands behind your back. I'm going to push James onto the bed, and I'm going to be the one to suck him off. You're just going to kneel here and watch." Al dug his teeth deeper into his lips and gave Laurie a pleading look. Watching Laurie and James together made him hard at any time; watching them now, when he was already turned on beyond belief, would be almost impossible to cope with without his hands on his cock. He'd burst with the need. Laurie relented. "All right, you can touch yourself. But only through your clothes and only with your right hand. You're to keep your left hand behind your back."

Al nodded, relieved. Laurie and James collapsed on the bed together. Laurie lay by James's legs, and Al watched the expression on Laurie's face as he looked at James's cock. Adoring, almost worshipful. Laurie always looked at it that way. Actually, he looked at James that way too—as if James was the most marvellous being in the world, and Laurie couldn't believe he actually got to be with him. It was rather touching, seeing how much Laurie loved James. But it hurt just a tiny bit now Al realised how much he himself loved both men. He could never imagine anyone looking at him quite like that. Laurie bent to take James in his mouth, and Al moved his right hand round to touch himself. It was weird; left-handed Al was used to his other hand, so there was a clumsiness involved in using this one, even to stroke himself through his jeans. It felt odd. Al suspected that Laurie had guessed it would, and the thought that Laurie had done this deliberately was curiously hot, making up for the awkwardness. James was lying back on the bed, surveying Al through half-closed eyes as his breathing became heavier and harsher under his boyfriend's ministrations. Heat went through Al at the thought of being watched touching himself, too. It was something which usually didn't come up in his encounters; there always being someone else to touch him instead. In Al's experience, either you were alone, or someone did it for you (or was at least too occupied to be staring at you). Certainly no one had looked at him with that particular expression in their eyes. Touching himself under James's interested gaze was a very different experience to anything Al had ever done—which, when you'd done as many things with as many people as Al had, was saying something.

Laurie's hands were playing with James's balls, reaching further back to tease at his entrance even as he took James deeper into his mouth.

James gave a little groan, hitching his hips up a bit. Laurie slicked one of his fingers with the saliva sliding down James's cock and pressed it against him, and James moaned again, his back arching off the bed a little way. Al's jeans were beginning to feel very uncomfortable against his erection; watching James lose control like this was a wonderful sight. Laurie's mouth worked faster, his finger pushing further into James, crooking to hit a certain spot inside him. And Al was stroking himself harder and harder as he watched, wondering whether he was going to come just like this, knowing he could do quite easily. But no, he wanted to know what Laurie would do with him next, so he pressed the heel of his palm hard against the base of his cock and squeezed his eyes closed for a few seconds. The latter didn't help. It just made him more aware of the little noises James was making, the squelch and suck of Laurie's mouth around James's hard cock. He opened his eyes again, taking a few deep breaths. He was in time to hear James groan one last time and then see him jerk and shake, watch Laurie swallow what he could of James's come, and let the rest trickle out of the sides of his mouth. God, his lovers were sexy. The eroticism of watching. Al had never much thought about it before he'd got together with them both, but when the men he was watching were James and Laurie, it was glorious.

"Undress, Al." Laurie's voice came across his thoughts, breaking his concentration. "Stay on your knees—as much as you can."

Al bent his head in acquiescence and stripped his T-shirt off in one flowing motion. Laurie, he saw, was now kissing James, but he had his eyes open and was watching Al at the same time. James was all loose and languid, smugly sated by his orgasm and happy just to lie back and enjoy himself. Al struggled to get the jeans over his hips. His cock was so very engorged that the material caught against it, and he made a small hissing noise between his teeth at the sensation of the zipper dragging against his erection. He felt rather than saw the warning glance from Laurie at the sound and reminded himself once more that he was supposed to be silent. Silent, fuck. How was he ever going to manage that? But the jeans were down to his knees now with his boxers, and he fumbled his way out of them without leaving the floor more than a couple of inches, pulling his socks off as he reached his feet. Then, naked, he returned to his submissive kneeling position, lowering his head and putting both hands behind his back as Laurie had ordered earlier.

"Gorgeous," Laurie said appreciatively. He undressed , briskly shedding the clothes onto the floor. "Now come up here, Al. Let me touch you."

"And me," James added, stretching lazily. "You're very pretty today, Al."

Usually, Al would respond to a comment like this with a swift "Fuck off" or other pithy retort of that nature. He suspected James of taking advantage of Al's instructions not to speak to say something like that. But it was surprisingly nice to be able to take the compliment—for James had certainly meant it, no matter his awareness of Al's usual lack of appreciation for such remarks—without denying it, or making light of it in some way. He could feel a faint blush creeping into his skin, warming his face.

"Kneel on the bed between us," Laurie said. "That's right."

Al knelt as both James and Laurie ran their hands over him in a possessive fashion. It took all his concentration to stop him from making soft noises of pleasure as they did so. Laurie's hands were firm and warm, James's gentler, teasing against his skin. He wanted to lean into the touches but forced himself to stay in position, doing his best to please his lovers.

"So hot like this," James said, his voice still smug from his earlier orgasm.

"Mm-hmm. Now, Al, I want you to kiss James. Show him how hot you thought he looked coming," Laurie said. "I know you did. I could see the way you were looking at him. Show him how much you needed to touch yourself, how hard you were just from watching him."

"Fuck, Laurie." James's face was touched with pink from embarrassment and renewed arousal combined.

Al leaned down to James, pressing his body against his lover's and putting his mouth on James's. Waited for James to respond before beginning to kiss him with ever-mounting passion because, fuck, Laurie was right. James had looked intensely hot as Laurie sucked him off. James, more languorous than on other occasions, melted into the kiss, allowing Al to control it and offer up everything he had.

"Mm, I can see it turned you on, you little slut," Laurie said, his voice warm and encouraging. "You'd be begging for it if you were allowed to talk, wouldn't you?"

At this, Al couldn't help making a little noise of want. He was so desperate—so desperate for *something*. He began to rut his body up against the side of James's, but Laurie caught his hips and held him still, preventing him getting any friction against his aching cock.

"No noise," Laurie scolded, "and no getting yourself off. I told you to kiss James, not fuck yourself against him. You need to wait for that." He ran the tips of his fingers over Al's erection, and the same noise squeaked from Al's mouth against his volition. He was powerless to stop it, no matter how much he wanted to bend to Laurie's will. "I'm going to fuck you in a minute," Laurie whispered into his ear, licking the edge. "You'll put your hands on the headboard and keep them there; let me take you as hard and fast as I like."

Al wrenched his head away from James, in order to say, "Yes, Sir," obediently, needing to say something, wanting to convey his need to Laurie through the pleading tone of voice.

Laurie laughed and let him kiss James a bit more before relenting. "Hands on the headboard, then," he said. "Spread your legs wide, Al. I'm not going to prep you. A bit of lube is all a slut like you needs to take me, isn't it?"

"Yes, Sir."

"James, any preferences for what you feel like doing?"

"Oh yeah," James said casually, looking up as Al moved into position. "I'm going to suck his cock for him. I'm sure Al will enjoy not saying anything, not making a noise as we take him together."

Al bit down hard on his lip. Even the thought was making him want to moan. James so rarely went down on either of his lovers, and the idea of his doing it now, when Al was forbidden to speak, forbidden to move without permission, was a sort of exquisite torture. He wanted to beg. He wanted to touch and kiss and groan and plead with his lovers, and he could do nothing but arrange himself, legs spread wide apart, hands holding tight to the wooden headboard, waiting for their pleasure.

"He looks good like that, doesn't he?" Laurie said to James.

Al knew that they were deliberately taking their time, making him burn up with need. He squeezed his eyes shut and clenched his hands even more tightly on the wood to a point that it was deliberately painful. He needed Laurie and James. He needed them so much.

"Not bad," James agreed.

He slid round on the bed so that his head was between Al's legs; Al could feel James's warm breath against the inside of his thigh. Al took a sudden indrawn breath at the sensation. He could hear the familiar sound of Laurie lubing his erection and nearly groaned in relief at the thought that he would soon have it inside him, remembering just in time to bite the noise back.

"I should take a photo, Al," Laurie said, "show you what a slut you look like this, begging to be fucked. Legs spread so wide, offering yourself up like that. Shameless tart that you are."

Al felt his cock throbbing at Laurie's words. He took some deep, steadying breaths, forcing himself not to break down and beg.

"You're such a tease, Laurie," James said, deep satisfaction in his tone. Al knew that James would say he deserved this for his deliberate incitement of Laurie. He trusted that the pair of them wouldn't force him to suffer too much more.

Laurie laughed. "I'd tease him longer, but he does look hot waiting here for me. I can't resist taking what's being so brazenly offered."

Al breathed a quiet sigh of relief at this and waited hopefully. True to his word, Laurie made no effort to prepare Al to be fucked, choosing just to rest the head of his cock against Al's hole and nudge gently against it. Al hissed out a breath, and James's warm mouth ascended to his cock at that second. Al jerked. It was too much after all the teasing. And yet still not enough; he was dying to be filled. He turned his head to one side, biting down hard into his upper arm to stop himself crying out. Laurie was slowly, slowly, *slowly* pushing into him, and the desire to thrust back against him was strong. Meantime, James was licking up and down Al's aching erection, bringing both pleasure and a building need.

Silence, Al chanted inside his head. *Silence, silence, silence. Don't speak, don't make a noise.* He stopped breathing altogether in an attempt to prevent any sound escaping his mouth; but as Laurie and James continued to suck and fuck him, he found himself taking a deep, hard gasp of air, which sobbed out of his lungs as he breathed out. He was still biting into his arm, knowing that he would have tooth-shaped bruises there in the morning and not caring. Laurie pulled out and thrust back in and Al moaned. He couldn't help himself. The moment the noise passed his lips, he felt ashamed—he'd had a direct order and hadn't kept it. James's mouth engulfed him, and Al threw his head back, panting, determined not to cry out again.

But the movements kept happening—James on his cock, Laurie inside him, and Al's control slipped a bit further. He bit back down into his arm even as another moan burst from his lips. Laurie ran a hand down his arm, gently removing Al's teeth from it and stroking the abused skin with his fingertips.

"Hey, no hurting my lover," he said, his fingers warm against Al, sending goosebumps up his flesh.

Al opened his mouth to assent, but James's mouth sucked him down to the root, and instead, he cried out loudly. Then he groaned again as Laurie pulled out and thrust back into him. Al was being torn apart by lust, but at the same time he was half despairing because he'd had his orders, and oh god, he wasn't keeping to them. His head dropped forward in shame.

"I'm trying to be quiet. I swear I am," he pleaded desperately. Disbelievingly, Al realised there were tears in his eyes. Somewhere deep in his head, he knew he was being ridiculous, but he couldn't help himself. He wanted so much to do as he'd been instructed, and he hadn't been able to manage it. He'd let them down. "I'm sorry. I'm so sorry."

"Shh, it's fine." James disengaged from Al's cock to speak words of reassurance, reaching up and touching his face, wiping a tear away from his cheek with a gentle finger.

Laurie, behind him, his cock still buried deep in Al's arse, put his arms right round him. "You're doing great," he said, his deep voice echoing right through Al. "Come on, love. It's okay. You can be as loud as you want now. You're doing great."

Al dashed away the tears with an impatient hand. "Stupid," he murmured.

"Such a good boy," Laurie said, kissing the side of his face, the back of his neck.

He began to move inside Al, just gently, and James returned his mouth to Al's cock, sucking it into his mouth and nuzzling it, swirling his tongue around the head. Al replaced his hands on the headboard and moaned, pathetically grateful to be released from the need for silence.

"That's it," encouraged Laurie. "As loud as you want. As loud as you need."

"Please..." Al keened, the word seeming to take forever to pass his lips.

"Yes."

Laurie continued to rock gently inside him, and Al couldn't stop moaning, couldn't stop the noises slipping from his mouth. Incomprehensible syllables, the names of his lovers, and finally just the word please over and over. Laurie began to move faster, and James, in turn, took more of Al's cock into his mouth, sucking on him until it was almost unbearable that his body could take so much pleasure. Al was crying out and shaking and pleading. He could feel the heavy weight of James's hand on his leg, the hot, sweaty body of Laurie against his back as his dominating lover thrust into him. The room smelt of arousal and sex and Al gave a long, harsh cry and started coming. It wasn't a moment. It was an eternity. It seemed to go on forever, his head whirling and his limbs shaking uncontrollably as his cock pulsed in James's mouth, and his arse spasmed around Laurie. Even when it finished, he was struggling for breath, his head sinking against the headboard of the bed between his hands as he panted and gasped. Laurie must have come at some point; Al's arse was wet and dripping, even as Laurie's cock was still inside it. At last, Laurie sighed and pulled out, gently unlatching Al's hands from their grip and pulling him down into the bed between himself and James, who wriggled over to make room.

"Sorry," Al whispered apologetically again.

"God, Al, you were amazing," James said, an arm flung firmly over his waist.

"Perfect." Laurie leaned in and kissed him.

"I messed up." Al wasn't sure whether he was more embarrassed by having cried, or having failed. Both, perhaps. He felt weirdly wobbly.

"You were so good," Laurie corrected him. "Trying so hard for us. Al, you were—"

"So fucking hot," James finished.

Al saw Laurie's eyes light up with amusement as they caught James's across his body. "Yes, that," Laurie agreed.

Laurie looked back at Al, running a strong hand over his side. The gesture was reassuring, firm. Something to hold onto when the world was spinning, just a bit. Al's heart rate was still racing, but his mind was beginning to return to him. He felt like he'd been a million miles away. They lay quietly for a few minutes.

"Al?" James said tentatively, at last.

"Shit," said Al, coming back to himself slowly. "Sorry. Don't know what came over me." He thought for a second. "Well, at least, I do, but—"

"Subspace," said Laurie quietly. Al nodded. "Have you done that often?" Laurie asked.

"No." Al swallowed. "I mean, I've...you know, done what I'm told a bit, like we've done in the past—played at it. But nothing like that." He flushed. "If you must know, I didn't really think it was a real thing. Not that—intense." He shivered slightly, reliving the feeling—the desire to give all of himself up to Laurie and James, just to be what they wanted him to be. The wonderful, head-spinning freedom of voluntarily offering up all control, everything you were, to somebody else.

"You okay?" James asked, leaning up on one elbow and looking anxiously at him.

"We don't need to do it again," Laurie added hastily.

"Yes" —Al corrected him, equally quickly— "yes we do. Geez, that was...incredible. I mean" —and there was still a shadow of the feeling, the shame of failure there— "I know I messed up, but—"

"You didn't mess up, Al," Laurie said. He gave a sudden, unexpected smile. "And I should know, after all," he reminded him. "If I say you were bloody brilliant" —and there was a hint in his voice, just the smallest hint, but a hint, of the deep, dominating Laurie who had emerged during the last hour— "then that's what you were." Then it was gone, and the normal, everyday, gentle, and caring Laurie was back. "You sure it's okay with you—what we just did?"

Al nodded. "I liked it. A lot."

He was used to being confident, sure of himself. Especially when it came to sex. Yes, he'd played about with doing what he was told—as he'd said, he'd done a certain amount of that with James and Laurie in the past, though not like this. He'd also played at dominating others, though giving orders had always been a bit of a laugh to him, whereas Laurie, it seemed, was a natural. Al felt a little tremor go through him, thinking about how it had felt with Laurie telling him exactly what he wanted, what he expected from him. It had been deeper, stronger than anything he'd ever experienced before. But though the others must not know it, this whole thing was like that. It was more than just sex. This was love. Al had never known anything about love and definitely not like this.

"Sure?" Laurie asked.

Al could feel James's eyes on him. He had a suspicion James knew more than Laurie about how much Al had...well, 'enjoyed' was not, perhaps, the right word...*needed* that release. Laurie, Al knew, was finding it difficult to see past the fact that he had brought Al to tears; Al wasn't sure he had the words to explain that it had been cathartic, wonderful. James gave him a little smile of understanding, and it gave Al the courage to go on.

"It makes me feel…" He hesitated, unable, nonetheless, to look at either of them. The word he kept trying to deny slid through his mind again, the one he'd spoken aloud for the first time to Gemma a couple of weeks earlier. "…owned," he finished, waiting for Laurie to scoff, for James to tease.

"And you—don't mind that?" Instead of mocking, Laurie's voice was tentative in return.

"Mind?" Al gave a little laugh of disbelief.

"God, Al, I thought you'd be furious with us—with me," Laurie corrected himself. "For wanting you like this." Laurie, it seemed, had his own demons to fight. An earlier Al might have teased at this point, but this one suddenly understood that there were some bits of oneself it was hard to discover. "I mean—I wouldn't want you that way all the time," Laurie added hastily. "But…"

"Sometimes." James finished for him. He gave Al a bigger grin this time. "You do know I came again just sucking you off, don't you? Watching you fall apart like that. Fuck, Al, the way you don't hold back…"

Al gave a sudden gurgle of laughter. "Told you I was good," he said. "Didn't know I was that good, though."

"You are." Laurie's warm tones washed over him.

Al was half embarrassed by how good it felt, but it was unusual for Laurie to be so forthcoming after sex. During, he might tell Al how gorgeous he was, but afterwards it was more usual for him to treat him with teasing tolerance. None of them were into flowery declarations—at least not in Al's presence. He didn't know, he thought with a slight pang, how Laurie and James were when they were alone together.

James proved his point. "We-ell, not bad," he drawled, eyes alight with amusement.

"Could say the same for you," Al responded immediately, the return to safer ground a relief, on the whole.

Nonetheless, Laurie hadn't quite finished on the subject. "So, not just a one-off?"

"God, I hope not." Al knew the sincerity in his voice shone through. If he hadn't been able to hear it for himself, he'd have seen it by the look in Laurie's eyes.

"And Alistair's okay—as a safeword?" Laurie checked. "If we're really going to do this again, I need to know you're all right."

"I'm not going to say it unless I'm very much not all right," Al, who hated his full name, muttered darkly. But he gave a reluctant smile. "Yeah, it's good. But...um...promise you won't stop if I don't say it?"

Laurie raised his eyebrows. "That sounds...interesting."

"Promising," James said with a grin.

Laurie laughed. "That too. Al, if you swear to me you'll safeword if you need to, I won't stop unless you do."

"Cross my heart," Al promised. "I'm not a masochist, and I don't have a death wish. Sorry if that's what you want and all, but no."

"I don't," Laurie assured him.

"So...that being sorted," said Al, stretching aching limbs idly. "Jamie, any chance of dinner...?"

CHAPTER ELEVEN

Gemma had managed to persuade Al to invite James and Laurie out to meet her. Al had found himself somewhat unwilling. It was unusual for him to introduce his sex partners to one another, though both Gemma and the other two had been with him for so long that they had, in fact, met before. But it felt weirder now, knowing that Gemma knew how he felt about his housemates. He felt embarrassed—self-conscious. However, she'd been very good on the occasions that the two of them had been together—sympathetic, and only a little teasing. To be honest, Al would have felt odder if she hadn't teased him at all. It would have brought home to him all too strongly how difficult and uncomfortable this new feeling was. So, half reluctantly, Al had suggested to Laurie and James that they come out for a few drinks at the beginning of an evening with Gemma.

"You can go home after a while," he assured them. "I'm not asking you to stay around all night—"

"I should think not," James had said, amused. "Neither of us do girls."

"Fuck off," Al retorted. "I didn't mean that as you well know. But she reckons—considering I'm living with you and all—if I wanted to bring her home, it might be good if she'd, well, said hello or something in advance. If you know what I mean," he added, trying to stay casual. The excuse had been Gemma's suggestion. It had sounded good when she said it, but it sounded like the...well...excuse it was when he said it out loud himself. Apparently it didn't come across that way to the other two however.

"Fair enough," Laurie agreed. "It sounds fine. You'll have to nudge James or something when you want us to leave. We don't want to cramp your style, after all." Al could see him biting back a smile.

"As you said to me when I moved in here," Al retorted, "don't worry about that—you won't. I'd hate to shock Jamie's delicate sensibilities by making out with a woman in front of him, however."

James snorted. "How many bloody girls have I seen you snog, Al Hitchins?" he demanded. When you'd known someone as well as Al had known James since the age of ten, there wasn't much they hadn't seen you do.

Al laughed. "See?" he said to Laurie. "Not a problem. Cool. I'll tell Gem. She'll be pleased."

"Who wouldn't be?" James murmured. "Me and Laurie—who could possibly resist a music teacher and a film lecturer when you're a famous singer...?"

Al gave him a two-fingered gesture and left. Nonetheless, he was grateful they didn't know how much Gemma quite literally was looking forward to meeting them. She'd sworn to be on her best behaviour and not give them any clue by word or deed as to Al's feelings about them. Al knew she wouldn't let him down, but he couldn't help being nervous, especially when the evening in question came around.

Laurie, James, and Al went to the pub together. Al had been in charge of timekeeping, so they were early, and Gemma wasn't there, which was almost a relief. Al could do with having his housemates safely ensconced with a drink by the time he (re)introduced them to Gemma. So James and Al made their way to a table whilst Laurie headed to the bar. Before they could get there, however, Gemma appeared.

"Hey, darling," she said to Al, kissing him appreciatively.

"Hiya. You remember James, don't you?" Al said, waving a hand vaguely at his best friend. "And Laurie's over at the bar."

"The big one."

Al gave Gemma a bit of a glare at this. "Yes. The big one," he said, with the faintest suggestion of gritted teeth.

She smiled at him and turned to James. "Hello, aga—" She cut off suddenly.

"What?" asked James—as well he might, Al thought. Gemma was staring at him as if she'd never seen anyone like him before. Was this her idea of subtle?

"Sorry," she laughed, seeing the slightly bewildered expression on James's face. "Was that terribly rude of me? It's just... Goodness, I'd forgotten how much you looked like Al." She continued to look him up and down. So it was not, in fact, that she'd never seen anyone like him before—but that she *had,* Al thought, ruefully amused. "I mean," she added, evidently noticing how much further she had to look up to take him all in, "apart from being—" She waved a hand upwards.

"Taller and fitter and more muscular, I know," said Al, butting in and rolling his eyes theatrically. "My poor bruised ego, Gem, for goodness sake. Can no one point out that I have vague facial similarities to James without then going on about how much better looking he is?" But he was grinning. They always had been taken for brothers, he and James, since they were kids. Al was often tempted to kiss James in public just to shock people. And it did explain Gemma's sudden deviation from the script.

"I think your ego will survive," Gemma told him, smiling back at him and kissing him on the nose—conveniently placed when they were so very much of a size, after all.

"Anyway, she can't help it if I'm just much more handsome than you are," James added immediately, also grinning.

"Though of course neither of you are as tall and fit as your boyfriend," Gemma added provocatively to James, looking at Laurie, who had turned from the bar with the round of drinks.

Both young men laughed at that. "There is that," James admitted. "But he's dating me, so I think I'll call that a win."

Gemma's eyes met Al's for a second, and he looked at her pleadingly. She nodded reassuringly at him.

"Sounds reasonable," she agreed, blandly, with James.

Al noticed that Laurie was getting close, so he raised his voice a little. "Terribly old, though," he said, making sure Laurie could hear. "Pretty decrepit, really."

Laurie dumped the drinks down on the table beside them and looked at Al with a glint in his eye. "Still able to keep you in order, though," he retorted. "I presume that was aimed at me, anyway. Can I get you a drink, Gemma, whilst I'm up?"

Al couldn't help a little smile at Laurie's first comment. He knew Gemma noticed and felt himself blush a little. She'd tease him later about that, he knew. But she was on her best behaviour, and the couple of drinks went well before James excused himself and Laurie; and Gemma, smiling, assured him that she was quite happy to do the same for herself and Al—"probably for the same reasons," she added. James choked and looked away. Laurie appeared amused.

"Quite possibly," he agreed. He glanced at Al. "Enjoy. Nice meeting you again, Gemma."

"I could say the same."

Gemma, Al thought grimly, could be extremely flirtatious when she chose. Not that it was something Al could precisely complain about. However, chatting up Laurie, his sometime lover and secret love, was a little unnecessary he felt. And, damn her, she knew he was thinking it. She stroked his leg as Al's two loves made for the exit—apparently to go home and shag.

"Sorry, darling," she said apologetically, "but I couldn't resist."

Al could never be cross with Gemma for long. She was too much like him. If the positions had been reversed, he acknowledged to himself, he would have been struck by the same temptation.

"Heartless wench," he retorted.

She giggled. "Why don't you take me home and put me in my place, then?" she suggested. "As I gather Laurie does to you."

"Now that," Al said, ignoring the second part of her comment and suddenly feeling considerably better about everything, "sounds like a very fine plan."

Which it would have been, except for a further demon that raised its head just as things were getting interesting. Gemma was straddled across Al's prone body, kissing his neck as Al's hands played with her breasts. She licked a path across his throat and then pulled back suddenly.

"Hey," Al objected, "what did you do that for?"

Gemma was frowning, running a finger across where her mouth had just been. *Oh. That.*

"You've got a scar," she said. "What'd you do—cut yourself shaving or something?"

"Yeah, I have a fetish for slitting my own throat," Al said ironically. "Thought you knew." He gazed up at her steadily. "Is now really the moment?" he asked.

She slid down his body so that she was lying on top of him, her face close to his. "It was just a frivolous question, but given that response, yes, I think I probably do need to know," she said seriously.

Al glanced away, repressing a shudder. "Someone attacked me," he said baldly—a deliberate understatement, but the nearest he could get to the truth. "A while back—just after you went away. It wasn't deep, but it got infected."

"What the hell...?"

Al shifted uncomfortably. He hadn't wanted to mention it, feeling ashamed about the whole thing. He felt crap about the way he'd done nothing when he'd been attacked. Though he'd underplayed it to Gemma, he knew well enough that the truth was that he hadn't been attacked by 'somebody' but by several somebodies. The trouble was he'd just let the men do what they wanted with him. Laurie and James had told him over and over that he had nothing to feel ashamed about, that there had been five of them—one with a fucking big knife—and only one Al, but it didn't entirely help. Though he'd been to the police, no one had ever been caught, and he was guiltily relieved that he wouldn't have to face his abusers...which made him feel like an utter coward all over again. He'd been beaten badly, after which the men had pushed him to the floor and then taken it in turns to shove their cocks in his mouth until he couldn't breathe, hissing slurs and threatening further violence as they did so. He hadn't even told James and Laurie about the worst parts of it in any detail—hadn't been able to. The episode still haunted him; he suspected it always would.

"If you must know, that's why I'm living with the other two," he said quietly. "Not because they want me there. Because I was attacked, and they thought I needed...I dunno. Minders. Another reason why I can't tell them about—well, you know. In fact, come to think about it, I ought to move out soon. It was never supposed to be forever, just for a bit."

"Oh, Al," Gemma said. She leaned down to kiss the scar. "I'm so sorry, darling." She looked at him with worried eyes. "That's a knife wound, isn't it? That's not someone playing about."

Al couldn't talk about it. Not even to her. "It was shallow," he said dismissively. "It was just the infection. Look, forget it."

She took a deep breath. "Okay. I'll try." She wouldn't forget, and Al knew she wouldn't, but he appreciated her respect for his privacy. She kissed him on the mouth in a very different manner. "But yes, I can see why that makes it difficult for you to tell Laurie and James you're in love with them. If you feel they don't really want you there anyway." She leaned back, looking thoughtfully at him. "Having seen them with you tonight, I'm not so sure that's true, but—"

"Trust me, the subject never came up before then," Al told her. "Would that it had. Fuck, I should move back out again, shouldn't I?"

Gemma sighed, and rolled off him. "Clearly, the moment is lost," she said regretfully. "Come on, let's go out for dinner. I can always bring you home and ravish you later. Until then, come and tell your Auntie Gemma all about it, and she will give you wise and sage relationship advice."

She stood up and stretched unselfconsciously before spraying body spray across herself and stepping into some extremely sexy knickers. Al admired the view even as he rued what had led to it. His eyes followed her appreciatively, but he said dismissively, "'Auntie' Gemma needs to learn that I don't do relationships. How many times, Gem? How many times?"

She stepped into her dress and smiled at him via the mirror on her wardrobe. "It worked so much better when you believed it yourself, honey."

And Al, for once in his life, had not a word to say in response to that.

CHAPTER TWELVE

"God... Fuck, *Jamie*..."

Al, sliding through the front door quietly five nights later, trying to make sure he didn't wake the other two, was caught by surprise by the words. Laurie and James had presumably expected that he was going to be out much longer, possibly all night. Hell, Al had thought he might be. Except that tonight's intended shag had drunk too much, and Al was not into taking advantage of adults too drunk to consent. He'd walked his would-be date home, seen him safe, and left him with a kiss on the doorstep. The gentleman in question would be glad in the morning—if he was able to remember anything at all. Al had assumed that Laurie, at least, would be asleep by now. Unlike James and Al, Laurie kept sensible hours by instinct, to the point that you'd think staying awake after midnight ran the risk of turning him into a werewolf or something.

Or something.

Judging by the noises in the room to Al's right, the hours after midnight did *something* to Laurie. This was like no version of Laurie that Al had ever met. Hoarse, begging. Really fucking hot.

Al was the loud one, James somewhere in between. Laurie didn't say much in bed. He liked to give orders, sure, or tell Al or James how gorgeous they were, but that was different. His breathing got heavy and fast as he came closer to coming, and he was occasionally known to groan a bit if things were steamier than usual, but this?

"Please, Jamie, fucking—god, yes, there. Yes. Oh god, please. James. James. Jamie..."

This was something new. Al leaned back against the front door, his cock hard and throbbing. He shouldn't be hearing this. He ought to go into his room now, close the door—find earplugs or something. Do anything but slump back with his hand reaching down to rub himself as he listened to Laurie give it all up for James. Jesus bloody Christ, Laurie was begging James. Begging him. And Al was not pissed, but definitely not entirely sober, and he'd just walked away from a gorgeous bloke who had stated his out and out willingness to have sex with him, and these were his sometime lovers. And fuck, but it was turning him on, listening to them.

Wet noises coming from the bedroom, and that meant James must have his mouth around Laurie's cock because no way could Laurie be making that much noise if he was sucking James off. And that was a novelty, too—Al would suck cocks all day and night with pleasure, and Laurie went down on James given even the slightest encouragement, but James was more reticent about giving blow jobs. After all the times they'd shagged, Al could probably count on the fingers of one hand how many times James had sucked him. Once recently, granted, and Al would love to think that he had suddenly turned James on to blow jobs, but...

"Please. Oh god, please. Please."

Laurie begging. James sucking cock. Al had come home to a parallel universe, and it hit him like a blow, even as he shoved his hand inside his trousers despite himself and started wanking, how much he didn't belong here. Laurie and James... They had something special. Something Al didn't share. Sure, they took him in—like a stray animal—from time to time, but they didn't need him. What they had between them was a magical, private thing. And even though Al had known it, he hadn't *known* it, not like this. Not 'til he heard what it was like between them when they thought they were alone. Laurie's voice had softened in volume, and he was letting loose with a string of expletives so vulgar, so unlike him, that Al found his hand working faster than ever on his prick. He could hear James moaning— moaning—around Laurie's cock, and it was such a fucking turn-on. He heard the moment Laurie orgasmed, and that was it, Al was coming in his trousers like a bloody teenager.

The moment it was over, he felt disgusted with himself. God, for fuck's sake, like he couldn't get enough sex of his own. Did he seriously have to stand here, wanking to his best friends fucking? How bloody sick was that? He could hear the soft sounds of James and Laurie kissing, and desperate to keep silent, he slunk across the living room, opening his own bedroom door and closing it behind him. He winced at the loudness of the click it made as the latch caught. There was no way the others would have heard that, even if they'd had ears or brain for anything but each other, but in Al's guilty mind it sounded as loud as a drum crash. He pulled his hand, sticky with come, out of his pants and frowned at it with distaste. He'd been called a wanker on many occasions but none so accurately as this. Hating himself, he stripped off his clothes, wiping himself down with the tissues he kept by his bedside. No way was he going to the bathroom, not when Laurie or James might be out any moment on the same mission. Wishing he had whiskey in his own room and could drink himself into the same sort of stupor his would-be date was probably experiencing by now, he flung himself on the bed face down and tried to think about anything but what he'd just overheard.

☆☆☆

By the next morning, though, he knew the score. He really needed to move out. Sure, Laurie and James had said six months, but it had been five now, and Al had yet to start searching for a new place of his own. He hated how much there was a solid lump in his stomach at the thought. He'd always believed he liked living alone, had been grateful he'd not had to live in a shared house since university even if his bedsit had hardly been the height of luxury. Not like Laurie and James's flat, certainly. But Al knew, even as he thought this, that it wasn't the attractiveness of the flat which made him unwilling to leave. It was the attractiveness of the people living there. He'd live, he thought ruefully, in a bloody tent with these two guys if they wanted him.

The thought made him snort. He tried to visualise his two tall, strapping lovers attempting life in a tent, and wondered, with the first grin since he'd left his bloke on the doorstep the previous evening, how long it would take before James was threatening to strangle himself or someone else with a guy rope. Then he imagined Laurie marking student essays on a camp bed, hunched up so that he didn't touch the canvas with his head and ruin the waterproofing. The images helped Al regain his mental balance well enough to push open his bedroom door. He'd have to face the other two at some point, and after all, what they didn't know wouldn't hurt them. A bit of accidental voyeurism or the auditory equivalent (and rather less accidental wanking) didn't have to be the end of the world. *No*, his mind said sadly, *just the end of the house sharing*.

"Oh, shut up," he muttered to himself in irritation and realised that he was facing a somewhat amused James, who was sitting on the sofa.

"Usually I have to say something in order to be on the end of your morning grumpiness," James said, grinning at him. "Especially to be told to shut up. But apparently not this morning. Last night's fuck not to your taste? What time did you get in, anyway?"

Al ignored the last question. "Didn't have one, thanks," he said, shortly.

James raised his eyebrows. "What, he—she—they—zie—turned you down? I thought that never happened?" he drawled.

"Fuck off," Al said, without rancour. When you'd known someone as long as he'd known James, you didn't need to watch your language. "I turned him down, more or less."

"Curiouser and curiouser. Do tell."

Al shrugged. "Nothing to tell. He was pissed. Could hardly stand, let alone think about what he might or might not want. Saw him home—wasn't sure he could get there on his own, to tell the truth—and came away."

"Ah." James nodded. "That's why you're in such a foul mood this morning. Sex-starved. Poor Al. I made some coffee—proper stuff, decent stuff. It's on the side."

Al made his way to the bathroom, glaring at his friend as he passed. "For your information, I can manage the odd night without sex." Unlike you and Laurie, he thought, but did not add. "But coffee sounds good. After a shower. Where's Laurie?"

James sighed, stretched, and stood up. "Work, of course. Where I'll have to be in an hour or so. Where else? These people with grown-up jobs, you know. You shower. I'll reheat the coffee. The things I do for you, Al; the things I do for you."

And the things he did for Laurie, Al thought, turning the shower to cold as he tried not to relive the scene from the night before. Al knew sure as hell which things he'd prefer. By the time he was out and dressed, James had a cup of steaming coffee.

"Thanks," Al said, reaching for it.

But James was in a teasing mood this morning. Taking advantage of his several inches more height, he held it above his head out of Al's reach. "What are you going to do for it?" he asked.

Al blinked. "What? Oh, for fuck's sake, Jamie, just give me the bloody coffee."

There was a mischievous smile on James's face. "Persuade me."

"I'll jolt your bloody arm, and you'll have hot coffee all down it. That might persuade you," Al grumbled.

"What's it worth? A please? A kiss?"

"You're wanting me to do sexual favours for my coffee? Jamie, do you know how mad you sound?" Al asked. "Also, can you imagine what you'd do to me if I tried this on you?" James before his first coffee of the morning was not someone to mess with.

"I'm waiting," James reminded him.

Al glared for a second but was suddenly seized with an equal spirit of impishness. Going up to James, he slid his arms sensually around the other man, pushing his body up against him and raising his mouth to James's.

"Please, James," he whispered, his tongue tracing round James's lips before tentatively licking them open.

He pressed his mouth against James's, using every skill he knew to seduce him. And it was working; James had put his non-coffee-holding arm around Al, and Al could feel a growing bulge in James's trousers where they were pressed together. He undulated against it, and James let out a soft moan. Then, with a grin, Al made a grab for the coffee, taking James by surprise, and stepped away, triumphant.

"You little sod," James said indignantly, rubbing a hand against his suddenly deserted erection.

Al laughed. "Serves you right. Now, have you seen the local paper? I want to have a look for bedsits."

James paused. "You're joking, right?" he said, uncertainly.

"Thought it was about time I found my own place again," Al said. "I've been here five months."

"Look," James said awkwardly, "if this is punishment for teasing you about the coffee, I'm sorry, okay? Or if...you know, I'm that bloody annoying...I can stop being. I was only having a laugh."

"No, no, nothing like that," Al reassured him, trying to keep his own voice bright and breezy as if he were looking forward to the change. "But you and Laurie need your house back. It was only supposed to be for a bit, wasn't it? Oh, there's the paper." He had spied it underneath the television and went to get it, tugging it out.

"Okay." James's voice was unexpectedly cool. "Well, good luck. I'm teaching shortly, so I'm just going to go and look through my notes. Have fun house hunting."

CHAPTER THIRTEEN

The house hunting became a bit like the elephant in the room. James's immediate coldness about it had turned to an occasional mild question about how it was going. Laurie said, "I gather you're thinking of leaving us, Al?" in a questioning tone of voice, and when Al acquiesced, said, "Pity. I thought it was working quite well," in such a disinterested tone of voice that Al bloody nearly lost the will to live. Of *course* Laurie wanted his house and his boyfriend back to himself, but it had just been tough to hear it vocalised quite so blatantly.

Al scoffed at himself later. What had he expected—that Laurie would turn round and say, "Oh, please don't leave, Al! We love having you here. You make our life worthwhile"? And whilst it had clearly taken James by surprise, and maybe even upset him a little to begin with to hear that Al was considering making the move, he hadn't exactly been falling over himself to persuade Al to stay. Tonight, for the third time this week (so far), Al was staying in. Gemma wasn't free until the weekend, and Al hadn't got another late shift at the wine shop until the following night. He couldn't quite be arsed to go out and see if he could pick someone up—it just seemed like it'd be nicer to hang around at home with James and Laurie. Maybe watch a film, have dinner together. If he was going to be moving out soon anyway, it couldn't do that much harm if he stayed in a bit more often, could it?

"You're not going out?" James asked when Al mentioned that he hadn't got plans.

Al shrugged. "'Not tonight, Josephine.'" He cocked an eye at James. "Why, trying to get rid of me, Jamie?"

There was something painful in the way James had asked the question—as if he'd been expecting...worse, wanting...Al to sod off out.

"You're the one who wants to leave," James said. "No, I just thought you hadn't been out much lately. Anyway, it's Laurie who's out tonight, so it'll be just you and me."

"Like old times?"

"'Cept I'll have to do the cooking. Mum's not going to turn up. Actually, that's where Laurie's going."

"Bit weird really, isn't it? You know, your mum and your boyfriend being best friends."

James swung his leg back and forth. "Not really. I've never known anything different. And before you say that's a bit weird too, can I just remind you that you've not been in a relationship since you were eighteen, so you're not exactly in a position to comment."

"Geez, James," Al objected, "give me a chance to criticise you before leaping down my throat, why don't you? Fine. Fine. It's not at all weird that you're fucking your mother's best friend. Not at all." He flicked a glance at him. "Just hope they don't talk about sex as much as we always have."

James glared at him. "Don't go there, Al. Anyway, as you might have noticed, I'm fucking *my* best friend as well." He stood up and stretched. "I'll get some wine. Let's just admit that we're both completely messed up and leave it there, yeah?"

Al laughed. "Sounds good to me. Both parts of that."

"Come into the kitchen. I'll start cooking. Any preferences?"

James always asked that. Al wished he wouldn't—Al never really thought about food. Loved it, especially James's cooking, but thinking about what to eat? If it didn't come in a packet, Al was baffled.

"Whatever there is," he said vaguely, following James through and collecting glasses and wine. "I'm going to be drinking red wine, though, so if you're going to fuss about matching, then you can bear that in mind."

"Trust you to be more interested in the alcohol." James sounded resigned. "Okay, I'll make what I make."

"It's always good. You know that. Hmm..." Al slumped down at the table and poured some wine for them both. "Bugger, I suppose that means I'm on the washing up if Laurie isn't here."

"He is good for some other things apart from washing up, you know," James pointed out.

Al grinned. "I'd noticed."

James glared, picking up one of the glasses and taking a long sip. "Not just that. One track mind, you have."

"I don't know what you mean," Al said innocently. He cast a mischievous glance at James. "You're the one who leapt to that particular conclusion, not me. I merely said I'd noticed he wasn't just good at washing up."

"Tosser."

"Wanker."

James made a disgruntled noise, put down the glass, and started banging about in the fridge, hunting for food. Al was amused—this really was like old times. All it needed was Gillie to tell them not to break the TV if they started a fight, and it would be like being fifteen all over again. Except that he hadn't been ogling James's arse as he bent over in those days. Or perving over James's boyfriend, come to that. Fuck, when had life got so complicated? Though, to be fair, it hadn't exactly been a bundle of laughs all the time back then, either. Not with James coming out to Al as gay, and then developing a frankly embarrassing crush on a completely unattainable friend of his parents. Laurie had been twenty-six to James's sixteen—*and* involved in a long term relationship with another man. Now Laurie and James had been together longer than that previous relationship had lasted. Bloody hell, that was a weird thought, as well. No, now Al thought about it, Jamie's life had got a lot simpler since then... It was only Al's which was falling apart around his ears.

"Al?"

Al blinked, and looked up. Apparently James had said something to him, whilst he'd been lost in a brown study. "Sorry, what was that?"

"Are you okay?" James asked.

"Fine. Why?"

James had clearly found something to cook; he had out saucepans and a vicious looking knife. "Just...you're not out with one of your sex hook-ups; you didn't hear what I was saying; and most shocking of all, I'm drinking faster than you are. Something is clearly wrong."

Al flushed. Was he seriously so transparent? (Like his film. Except not. *Oh, do shut up, brain,* Al thought irritably.) "There's nothing wrong," he said, picking up his wine glass and taking a long swig. He couldn't exactly go out even if he wanted to (which he didn't); and he couldn't travel back in time and hear what James had said. What he could do was get drunk, and it was looking like a better idea by the minute. "What are you cooking?"

James rolled his eyes. "That's right, concentrate on the important matters, why don't you?"

"What, drinking and food? Hell, yes!" Al took another drink of wine, and James gave a reluctant smile.

"Barbecue ribs and pan-fried veggies, you idiot," he said. "And if something isn't the matter, at least pretend you're vaguely interested in what I'm saying, okay?"

Al gave him a mock salute. "Okay, captain."

The evening perked up a bit after that. James was enthused about a couple of new music students he'd taught a couple of times, and talked about them in depth. Al loved how keen his friend was on teaching, and the different things which thrilled him. For one of the students, it was the only part of the week where they were told they did anything well—the poor kid had been thrown out of school for bad behaviour (James suspected a learning disorder, but he wasn't in a position to say); the other was talented beyond any of the other people James taught, and James raved about her natural instinct to spot songs with the same or similar chord sequences and then play them one after another.

"It's amazing," James told him. "Did you know that 'Wings' by Birdy has the same chords as 'Yellow' by Coldplay? Because I didn't! But she played them to me, and she's quite right; it's the same chords in the same sequence, pretty much. You could do something incredible with a mash-up between the two."

Plus, two more students meant a couple more hours that James wasn't working in the music shop attached to the school. Al knew James was good at his work there, but it didn't have his heart the same way teaching did. The same way composing did.

"Have you got anywhere with music for *Transparent*?" he asked at length, when they'd finished eating and were sitting around on the sofa.

James gave the uncertain twitch that Al knew so well. It meant that he had something, but as always with James, he wasn't sure how good it would be. Which was ridiculous—in *Welding the Night Away*, Al's last film, the music had been specifically mentioned in more than one review. Actually, it had been mentioned more times (Al couldn't help but notice) than the directing had. Yet James was still so self-conscious about it that he wouldn't even allow Al to add his name to the credits, just running them under JAC, his initials. And Al knew that James still rarely composed or played his compositions in front of Laurie. James had always had a thing about how Laurie hated his guitar, from his earliest university days. In fact, it had turned out this inaccurate belief stemmed from the days before they started dating but were both interested in each other—Laurie extremely unwillingly, feeling it thoroughly inappropriate to be fantasising about his best friend's son. Watching James play the guitar had turned Laurie on more than he was comfortable with so that he had had to go away before the extent of his arousal had become clear. Laurie had confessed this once, red-faced and humiliated, to Al. He'd assured Al that James knew all about it, but from the way James acted, you'd think that James still thought Laurie couldn't stand his playing.

"I guess," James said reluctantly.

Al jerked his head towards the row of guitars that James owned. "Go on then."

"Hang on a sec."

James downed the rest of his glass of wine first, and Al, when James's back was turned, shook his head. For someone so talented, his best friend was horrendously lacking in self-confidence. With a deep breath, James picked up his favourite instrument and began to strum. Al's attention was caught immediately. It would have been anyway; anything to do with his film was sacrosanct. Al could never admit it, but he cared about his film-making like he cared about nothing else on earth. At least, like he'd cared for nothing else until he'd fallen so hard for Laurie and James. Al tried to shut his brain off, tried to kill the little voice that told him they mattered now even more than film-making. It was easy enough to do with James beginning to move into another piece. It was beautiful—haunting. It made Al want to shiver just listening to it. Sad, but ultimately uplifting, it was precisely the mood Al was aiming for with the film itself.

"Fuck, but you're good, Jamie," Al said appreciatively, almost involuntarily.

James ignored him, continuing to play. The notes trickled through Al as if they were alive. He could almost feel his story coming to life in the music. God, he was a sentimental idiot sometimes. Finally, James drew to a halt. They were both silent for a moment.

"Yes," said Al at last, unable to find the words for what he was thinking.

James looked up from his guitar uncertainly. "Yes?"

Al nodded. "That." He stood up and went over to James, kissing him gently on the lips. "You really read it, didn't you?" he asked softly. "My script."

James nodded. They looked at each other for a few seconds, the silence filled with all the things neither of them could say.

"Thank you," said Al, finally.

"It's okay?"

"It's...more than okay." Al pulled himself together. "The third part—a bit too soppy. A bit more harsh chords, maybe, there? It's not all smooth edges if you know what I mean. Ellie, the teenager, she struggles sometimes. Jack's a bit—well, he has his moments, you know? It's not easy trying to cope with it all."

James nodded. "Yeah. That makes sense." He looked down at the guitar again, played a short section as it had been before, and then changed it. "Something like that. Not that—that was too obvious. But—"

"Yes." Al turned away and went back to his seat. Stupid to be blinking away tears. He knew he was an idiot where his films were concerned—and an idiot where James was concerned—okay maybe it wasn't so surprising after all. Fucking emotional ponce that he was. "I think you've got the gist, anyway," he said, forcing himself to speak lightly. "Won't need it 'til later—got to get the actual filming done before I can put the music to it where it's needed. But yeah. Thanks." His eyes dry, he turned back. "For what it's worth, James, I don't use you because you're my mate. I use you because you're bloody talented," he said.

James huffed a laugh, and Al knew that he didn't really believe him. "Well. Thanks." He put the guitar aside.

"Oh, come here," Al said, going over to him and sitting across his lap, hugging him. "You're not half-bad, you know."

He straddled James, kissing him gently to start with and then a little more firmly. James kissed back, his arms pulling Al closer. Al wriggled closer still, wanting to be as near as possible to James, until the two were groin to groin, and Al found himself rubbing up against James and half groaning into his mouth as the kiss continued. God, James...

"Fascinating what happens when I leave the house," someone commented from behind Al.

Al shot back a few inches at the sound of the voice. Laurie. They hadn't heard him come in. He looked uncertainly at the other man, unsure of how he would feel about what he'd just seen. Whilst kissing James in Laurie's absence was not in itself problematic in the slightest, it was understood that neither James nor Laurie would have sex with Al in the other's absence. Al wasn't entirely sure whether the way he'd been grinding against James crossed the rather grey line between acceptable and unacceptable. James hadn't precisely been stopping him, but Al knew that he had been responsible for the more intimate parts of their embrace. However, Laurie didn't look too pissed off, and James seemed remarkably unbothered.

"Hey, Laurie, good evening?" James asked, his hands still resting gently on Al's back.

Laurie flashed him a smile. "Not bad. Gillie sends her love. Now, where were we? Ah yes." He glanced back at Al, who nonetheless waited with a small amount of trepidation. "Well, Al, hot as you look snogging James, I can't help thinking that you'd look even hotter naked and on your knees."

Al could feel his heart suddenly beating very fast. Although they'd had sex a few times since his first experience of subspace, it had been in the normal fashion. This, though...this sounded like Laurie was in a mood to dominate, and fuck but that turned Al on.

"Now...Sir?" he asked tentatively.

There was a predatory look on Laurie's face that boded well. "Oh, I think now; don't you?" he purred. "You appear to be in the mood for something—you and James." Feeling slightly discomfited by that last sentence, Al slid rather sheepishly off James's lap, uncomfortably aware that he was sporting a definite and rather obvious erection. Laurie looked him up and down possessively. "Clothes off," he ordered.

Al scrabbled with his T-shirt, making a bit of a hash of getting it over his head, and then dumping it onto a chair. James moved to the sofa and leaned back in a corner of it, his eyes on Al as Al's hands fell to his waist, and he unbuttoned his trousers. There was a hot, prickly silence in the room that made Al more than usually self-conscious. Unable to meet his lovers' eyes suddenly, he looked down as he stripped the rest of his clothes off. Laurie strolled over to sit next to James on the sofa, and Al came to kneel in front of them, hands behind his back, his gaze still on the floor. For a few electric seconds, he waited in silence. Then Laurie put out one hand and ran it over the side of his face and onto his shoulder before withdrawing.

"I was right. You really do look fucking sexy kneeling there obediently," Laurie said, his voice a caress. Al could almost *feel* his words against his skin. "Just think, James and I could sit here and wank all over you, cover you in our come, and then make you stay there on your knees, all despoiled and filthy, until we recovered. Then we could push you right down onto the carpet and take it in turns to fuck you so hard and fast that you'd come without anyone even touching your cock."

Al gave a little moan. Never mind coming without anyone touching his cock; if Laurie went on talking like this, he might come without anyone touching him at all. His cock was throbbing at Laurie's words. James clearly felt similarly; he'd flicked open his trousers and started touching himself with little repetitive strokes. Laurie flicked a glance sideways at his boyfriend and continued.

"Or we could tie you to the bed, all open and on offer for us," he went on. "Touch you all over. You could suck Jamie's gorgeous cock as I ran my hands and mouth all over your body. Grazed my teeth against your nipples, fucked you slowly with my fingers until you were begging to come. But we wouldn't let you. James and I would fuck right on top of you, and you'd just have to lie there, and we'd wait until you were crying and pleading before we'd let you get off."

"Bloody fuck, Laurie, *I'm* going to come if you go on like that," James said, his hand working faster on his cock, his trousers and pants shoved further down hastily, out of the way.

Laurie gave a little smile. "Or you could kneel on the floor here and watch me take James apart, inch by inch on the sofa, until he was so hot and desperate," he suggested, still speaking to Al but watching James as his breathing began to falter. "'Til he was the one begging, and then do you know what I'd do, Al? I'd give him *you*. You'd be Jamie's, to do whatever he wanted with, whatever he needed. Anything he wanted, you'd do for him. Would you like that? You looked like you'd like that, the way you were rubbing yourself off against him when I came in. Would you like to spread your legs for James and let him act out all of his dirtiest fantasies? Be his little fucktoy?"

James gave a groan, leaned forward towards Al, and came, splattering Al's face and chest with his seed. Al could feel it running down his body, and Laurie was right; he felt both so dirty and so turned on, dripping with James's come, feeling the first droplets sliding down to hit his hot, hard cock.

"Apparently James likes the thought of that." Laurie's voice was amused.

"Fucking tease," James said, breathing heavily and kicking his trousers off entirely. He leaned back again as if he needed the support of the sofa.

Laurie knelt down beside Al, dragging two fingers through the mess on Al's chest and then inserting them into Al's mouth. "Pretend it's

James's cock. See, it tastes of him, doesn't it? Doesn't he taste good, hmm?"

He slid his fingers back and forth between Al's lips, and Al's eyes flickered closed. Laurie was so fucking hot when he was like this; it was almost unbearably good. Al sucked greedily on the fingers, swirling his tongue around them. It was nearly like having a cock between his lips, especially with the taste of James's spunk on them.

"I want to see you take Al to the edge." James's voice drifted through into Al's consciousness.

Laurie laughed. "And what James wants... One of your dirty fantasies, love?" He removed his fingers from Al's mouth, and Al opened his eyes regretfully. He met Laurie's gaze. "Lie on the sofa, little slut," Laurie said.

Al crawled his way up to the sofa, lying down on his back with his head resting on James's knee. James's hand, almost instinctively, went to stroke his hair. James knew how much Al liked that; it made him want to stretch and lean into the gesture, catlike. Laurie knelt by the side of the sofa and dragged his fingers through James's come once more, returning them to Al's mouth.

"You liked that, didn't you?" he murmured, sliding his other hand onto Al's thigh and touching it with gentle fingertips. "You want to suck James's come off my hands, imagining you've got his cock in your mouth. Such a cockslut, Al. Such a pretty, filthy, cockslut that you are."

Al moaned around his fingers, Laurie's words going straight from his brain to his groin. The tiny, almost tickling, motions Laurie was making on his inner thigh were helping to move him into a state of shameless arousal, too. He sucked harder on the hand at his mouth.

"See, but I don't blame you," Laurie said, his tone low and intimate, "because it's James." Al felt Laurie lower his head to Al's chest and lick a stripe across it, licking up the last drops of come from one area before fastening his teeth around Al's nipple and giving it a little tug. "And when it comes to James," Laurie added, his voice so quiet Al could hardly hear him; his mouth licking further down, gathering up more sticky liquid from Al's body, "really, I'm quite the cockslut too."

Laurie's mouth was so close to Al's cock that he could feel the warmth of Laurie's breath against it. Heated breath with heated words that made Al buck up against him, trying to get some sort of friction against his cock, knowing better than to move his own hands to touch himself.

Behind him, he could hear James muttering something obscene about Laurie's language; he was pretty sure James was beginning to get hard for a second time just on the sound of Laurie's voice. Al couldn't blame him; he himself was beginning to go almost mad with desire. Laurie continued to clean Al up, his fingers still sliding in and out of Al's mouth as his warm tongue touched and teased the planes of his belly. Al knew he was making a pathetic whining noise, but he couldn't help himself. He was desperate to have his cock touched, and despite his best intentions, he began to slide his hand towards it, unable to bear not to any more.

The hand on his thigh reached out and grasped it firmly.

"You know better," Laurie scolded, pushing Al's hand up so that it was by his head. "James, hold on to the slut's hand for me. Apparently he can't keep control of himself."

Al whimpered something around Laurie's fingers that might have been "Sorry" and might have been "Please"—both words were buzzing in his head. James curled warm fingers around his lower arm and shifted underneath him a bit so the side of Al's head was resting against a definitely-not-entirely-quiescent cock. Laurie licked the last few droplets of James's come from Al's cock, and Al cried out, hoping that Laurie would continue—it wouldn't take much more for him to come.

But Laurie's mouth was gone almost as soon as it had touched, moving further down. Warm against Al's balls, suckling on them. Laurie slid his fingers out of Al's mouth and trailed them, saliva-wet, down Al's chest. Then, when both hands were on Al's thighs, he turned Al a little so that his legs were either side of Laurie's broad body. Pushing them back, he moved his mouth lower still, to the sensitive area between Al's testicles and arse. Al hissed and arched back so his head was resting even more heavily in James's lap. Laurie's lips—mouth—tongue—were so warm, and his tongue tickled the sensitive nub towards the back. Al could feel himself clenching and unclenching his fingers in a desperate attempt to try not to move them down to his cock; the arm held by James felt branded where James's fingers lay against his skin, but the other one...oh god, he wanted to move that one so much.

And Laurie's tongue was now licking across the pucker of Al's arsehole over and over. James reached for Al's other hand, bringing it up to the side of Al's head. With a gentle gesture, he rubbed the back of Al's hand against his own erection with a repetitive movement.

"Fuck," Al murmured. "Fuck, fuck, fuck…"

"Not yet," James said, his tone amused.

He dragged Al's hand—the one not touching James's cock—to his mouth and slid the fingers in and out of its warm depths. And Laurie was still licking him open; Al could feel his arse relaxing and loosening, opening up for Laurie, practically begging for him. And he lost it.

"Oh god, please… Fuck… Please, so good, I can't… That feels so good, please Laurie, please, Sir, oh god, James…" The words tumbled out of his mouth, unstoppable, needy. "Please, god, I… Fuck, oh fuck, Jamie, oh please, Sir, please…"

He was wide open under Laurie; Laurie pressed his tongue to Al's entrance, penetrating him, and Al knew he was begging humiliatingly for Laurie, and he didn't care. His fingers were warm and wet in James's mouth; James's cock was hard against the back of his hand, and Laurie was—

Laurie pushed a finger inside him, curling it to press up against his prostate, and Al came, his cock untouched, words still babbling out of his mouth. If James had wanted to see him taken apart, he'd had his wish; Al was in pieces, conscious of nothing except his body and his lovers.

"Fuck," he said, breathing heavily.

Laurie smiled across at him. "Better?"

"Thank you," Al croaked, still struggling for breath. Then, before he could stop himself, he added, "Will you fuck me?"

Laurie patted his leg. "I shouldn't think you're up to it right now, Al. Just lie there. It's okay."

Al bit his lip, trying to find the words to explain how he was feeling—difficult when it felt like everything inside his brain had been scrambled by his orgasm. "I want… Please… Oh, please… I want you inside me. I want you to come inside me." Begging to be fucked. Begging for it.

"Sure?"

Laurie appeared anxious, like he thought Al was only wanting to do this for his sake. When Al was dying to be filled, desperate to have Laurie in him, filling him up, making him his.

"So sure," Al whispered.

"You're so gorgeous," Laurie said quietly. Al could see that Laurie was hard; his trousers bulged with the erect cock within them. He undid them and slid them off, touching himself as he continued to stroke Al's leg. "So fucking gorgeous."

He slicked his cock with Al's come, and Al felt his heart give an enormous thump at the sight of it. Knowing he was greedy, probably shameless, just as they told him so often, he looked up at James.

"Feed me your cock, Jamie," he pleaded. "Let me suck you. Fuck my mouth."

"Bloody hell, Al." James swallowed convulsively.

"Please. I want..." What did he want? He wanted to show them how much he loved them, how much he wanted them. Al clamped down on the words—Laurie and James didn't want to hear that. "I want to be your slut," he said instead.

"Christ, you and Laurie are going to kill me," James said under his breath, his hand going instinctively to his crotch. "I'm so fucking hard, Al."

"Fuck my mouth," Al urged again.

He let out a deep breath as Laurie pushed inside him. Laurie was so big, he could make Al feel so damn full. And James was moving from under Al's head, kneeling over him instead, pressing his cock so slowly between Al's parted lips. Laurie in his arse, and James in his mouth, god. Perfect. So fucking perfect. He sucked greedily on James, who gave a little groan at the feeling. Laurie was beginning to move inside Al, back and forth; James started to do the same thing, pushing his cock further into Al's mouth, still careful not to choke him.

Al discovered that he was indeed still quite sensitive from having come. Each of Laurie's movements sent little shivers through him that were almost too much, but which at the same time he wanted to go on and on. James was filling his mouth, and Al couldn't help the moaning noises he was making around James; but judging from James's harsh breathing, James didn't mind too much. It was impossibly wonderful. James was staring down at Al, a desperately needy expression on his face, but even so—even whilst James was feeling like that, he still cared enough to be gentle, not to push too hard or go too fast. He was allowing Al to move his head, dictate the pace.

"Fuck, Al, fuck," James muttered hoarsely.

"Mmm," Al agreed indistinctly, pulling back to swirl his tongue around the head of James's cock before sucking him deeply in again. He could feel Laurie's hands on his sides, all warm fingers and large, firm palms, and it felt so good.

Laurie swore softly under his breath and started coming. Al groaned harder at the feeling spreading inside him, and that was enough to start James off. Then they were falling into a mess of arms and bodies and limbs wrapped round each other, and Al could hear himself saying "Thank you, thank you," over and over again. It was as if the voice didn't belong to him; he couldn't stop it, couldn't say what he was thanking them for, just knew that he felt so fucking grateful that they should touch him and allow him to touch them like this. James went back to stroking his head, and Laurie was whispering to him, telling him how amazing, how good, what a beautiful, well-behaved slut he was. Al wanted to stay in this moment forever, protected by his lovers' arms, safe and owned and belonging.

CHAPTER FOURTEEN

After that, Al knew more than ever that he needed to move out. Because the longer he stayed, the more he was finding his life—his heart—getting bound up in Laurie and James. It was wonderful in the good moments, when they were together and having fun (both in bed and out of it), but sometimes—for example, the next time Laurie went to visit Gillie and said "I'll tell her how you are, James...Al, too," and it was clear that Al was so very much an afterthought—it sent ridiculous shivers of pain through him.

But the move had to be put on hold for a while, no matter the knowledge, because filming for *Transparent* began. It was impossible to think about moving—or anything else—once Al had started the actual practical part of the film. He knew he was a terrible flatmate, a terrible friend—a terrible everything when he was filming. Nothing else could impinge on his concentration but what he was doing. They were filming all day from early morning to late into the night, and when he got home, Al was busy poring through some of the video, scribbling over the scripts for the following day, thinking, concentrating, making changes. From time to time James forced meals upon him, insisting that he ate. Al knew it was meant kindly, but it was an irritation, a distraction from what he wanted to be doing. Nothing was important save the film.

He knew that other people found it hard to understand the change in him at these times, but in fact both Laurie and James coped much better with it than he had anticipated. The fact that the usually jokey, flirty Al had become a stress-driven workaholic apparently didn't disconcert them. Aside from making sure that he ate, James did not bother him, and neither of them made any comment or complaint about the fact that Al was usually awake for most of the night, pacing the sitting room and muttering to himself, or buried so deeply in his computer that he was oblivious to everything. They didn't even criticise on the occasion he jumped and yelled top volume when James, fetching himself a drink of water at 3:00 a.m., had dropped a glass.

The noise Al made had woken Laurie, and Al had felt like a prize idiot, but the other two had just laughed at him (rather sleepily) and suggested that occasionally sleeping might prevent him from this sort of thing. Al had been too embarrassed to admit that the timing had coincided with his going over a bit of script where Jack, his trans character, had his window broken by transphobic neighbours, and that Al had somehow believed that he'd brought the story to life. Maybe, he'd acknowledged sheepishly to himself when the others had gone to bed, he ought to get a bit more sleep. But it was difficult when the film was so close to being perfect, so near to the vision Al had in his mind. Max, the man playing Jack's character, was an emotional fit to the part such as Al could never have imagined. Thankfully Max hadn't gone through half of the torment Jack did, but somehow it was difficult to believe that he hadn't. The scene in which Jack came out to his daughter, telling her he was not, in fact, a woman, was heartbreaking: the film was shot not from Jack's perspective, but from his daughter Ellie's, and the byplay between his confused and terrified daughter, who believed she was losing her mother, and Jack, who had suffered so much before coming to this conclusion, had brought half of the crew to tears—Al included. Now, if only the rest of the film could live up to that promise...

That being the case, it would take something very important to distract Al's attention away from filming—and dealing with a house move that he didn't even, in his heart, want to make was not in that category. Al couldn't, to be honest, think of anything that was. At least until it happened.

The nightmare came after the fifth day of filming. The one thing which could distract Al from absolutely everything else. Stupid to be so terrified by a dream, but it was one thing to know that and another to feel it—especially when it seemed so real whilst he was in it. It was always the same dream, and it never failed to shake him up.

Al had fallen asleep on the sofa, his laptop still open in front of him. Suddenly, he was back where he had been in early February. The sound of his name.

"That's him. Hitchins."

A knife at his throat. The sudden moment when the man holding it changed his mind and gashed it firmly into his leg. Al felt the warm blood with as much shock as discomfort; it trickled down his trouser leg, sticky and painful.

"Do what you're told, or there'll be more."

The threat had been seriously made, and Al had the scars to prove it. The knife had a wicked six-inch blade with a jagged edge, and Al was scared. He was so fucking scared. Four other men around him. One twisted his arm hard behind his back.

Al did as he was told.

He found himself on the deserted Norton's Street, pushed up against a cold concrete wall as the men took it in turns to punch him over and over. They were mixed in age and race—from perhaps eighteen to forty-five. They'd said his name; this wasn't a random attack; this was personal. Personal—from a group of men he'd never met. And Al didn't even know what he'd done. He was to get the gist, though, from their comments.

"Faggot."

"Fucking whore."

"You'd open your mouth or legs for anyone, bitch."

"Whore."

"Pervert."

Al said nothing. Did nothing save try to protect himself from the worst of the harm. Even if he'd tried to fight back, the odds were against him—five to one, and a wicked-looking knife. His leg was seizing up where it had been cut, a red line of pain which kept his attention even over the bruises the fists of the other men were providing. He wanted to say "Don't" or "Why?" but the words wouldn't come. And he refused to plead, even knowing that was what they wanted; couldn't bring himself to give them that satisfaction. A punch to the side of his face sent him spinning to the floor, half dazed. He felt the knife slice into his throat as he fell and wondered if they were going to kill him. It seemed likely. He wondered if he'd care and realised that he did, passionately. Wondered if anyone else would care and wasn't sure they would. Stopped wondering anything as the boots and shoes of his attackers jammed into his sides and legs.

A hand in his hair, dragging him to his knees. The knife back at his throat, pressing deliberately into the shallow cut that was now there.

"Fucking whore, open your mouth," hissed a voice.

Al knew, despairing, what was coming. He shut his eyes, felt the waves of pain go through his body. The knife cut deeper; someone held his nose until he had to open his mouth to breathe.

"Use teeth and we'll fucking kill you, faggot."

It got vague, then. The word 'whore' repeated over and over. A series of cocks in his mouth, choking him, stopping his breath for a second before relenting and pulling back. Someone pissing on him. Until finally, the moment one man went too far, and he passed out. Coming to alone, lying in fuck knew what, his coat gone, his clothes ripped, feeling pain and fear like he'd never known. Shivering and sobbing, humiliated and terrified and so, so cold...

"Al... *Al.*"

"Huh?" Al blinked open his eyes, felt tears on his cheeks and sobs bursting out of his chest. James was on the floor by his side, hand on his face, a small lamp turned on that lit up the concerned expression on James's face.

"Fuck, are you okay?"

Al's heart was still pounding from the dream. When he was filming, he slept so rarely, but the sleep he got was miles deep, more vivid than at any other time. It felt real. He reached down to touch his body, then his neck, checking—stupidly, he would tell himself when he was more awake—for the bruises, the cuts. Not there. Only the ghosts. Only the ghosts and the scars on his neck and leg to remind him.

"Sorry," he said groggily, choking back a sob. "Did I wake you?"

"You were..." James stopped. Al could fill in the gap. Screaming probably. Something like that. He didn't want to know, and James knew it instinctively. "Doesn't matter," James said. "You're okay."

"I'm fine," Al lied.

"Yeah." James's half smile told Al he knew it was a lie. "Come on, bed. Laurie's sleeping like a baby next door."

He tugged Al to his feet, and half led, half carried him into Al's bedroom. Then, without saying anything more, James lay down on the bed with him, curled his body around Al's, and went to sleep.

James was still sleeping when Al woke a few hours later. Unendingly grateful for his best friend's silent comfort, he slithered out from beside him. James slept deeply—Al had no idea how he had woken to hear Al's distress, unless it was the instinct of friendship which had led him—so there was little risk of waking him. Rubbing his face, and realising he was still dressed in the clothes from the day before, he stumbled out towards the kitchen for a drink. Water, coffee—something to hydrate him. He was due back to filming in an hour, he noticed; barely time to dress and get his things in order. Bugger it.

Belatedly, he noticed the kitchen wasn't empty. Of course, Laurie would have work. God, Laurie got up at this time every day, Al realised. Like most of the world, obviously. Perhaps it was James and Al who were the strange ones, still leading student-style lives of late mornings and late nights, albeit keeping up jobs nonetheless. Al could live with that, to be honest.

"Hey Al," said Laurie, pouring coffee. "Seen James?"

"Yeah, he's asleep in my bed," Al said, unthinkingly. Laurie raised his eyebrows, and Al felt himself going pink as he realised how that sounded—and then went pinker still at the thought that his blush was only likely to confirm Laurie's thoughts. "Erm, I mean...not like that...that is..." He stumbled to a halt, scared of making things worse if he said any more. He'd been sleeping with James—but not *sleeping* with him.

Unexpectedly, Laurie smiled. "I didn't imagine it was," he said. "Though I was thinking that possibly we might rethink that clause—still, not much point if you're moving out. It just seemed a bit daft when we're all living here together."

Al gave him a startled look. He had not imagined that there was any situation ever in which Laurie would be all right with James and Al having sex alone. Granted, there had been that one time when Laurie and he had fucked without James—though, to be fair, James had been asleep in the same bed as them. However, that had been under exceptional circumstances. The same exceptional circumstances which had, indirectly, led to James's presence in his bed last night, Al thought ruefully.

"Oh," he said faintly.

"So, out of a matter of interest—do you want a coffee, by the way—what *is* James doing in your bed?" Laurie asked casually.

Al grinned. "Sleeping." Laurie glared at him, and Al relented. "If you must know," he confessed, somewhat sheepishly, "I fell asleep on the sofa last night and had a nightmare. I think Jamie was sick of me screaming or something because he came and woke me up. Then took me back to bed like I was a five-year-old, and he was playing daddy."

Laurie snorted at this touching description. "Sounds like James." He poured Al a cup of coffee, but instead of giving it to him, he put it down next to his own and went over to Al. "Nightmares, Al?" he asked softly, folding his arms around Al.

Al tried to shrug it off. "It happens."

"Often?" Laurie asked, eyes anxious.

"No," Al lied. "It's just—"

Laurie cut him off by kissing him. It was a tender, loving kiss—passionate, for Laurie was incapable of kissing without passion, but gentle. Al felt himself melt into it, feeling protected in the same way he had when James had wrapped his body around Al's last night. He hated the thought of living without them; it felt as if he were going to have parts of himself ripped away. And that, of course, was why it had to be done, and the sooner the better. He didn't belong here, no matter how much he would have liked to. He was the spare wheel, the odd one out.

Laurie pulled away and ran a hand down Al's cheek. "I'm glad James was there for you," he said simply and turned back to the coffees.

Back on set, however, it all faded away. Nightmares, Laurie, James... When Al was filming, he was oceans deep in what he was doing. There were the practical issues—cameras, lighting, movements to sort out. But there were also the interpersonal ones. Working the hours they were doing, everyone was tired and on edge, which led to frayed tempers. Al was kept busy by a running feud between one of the lighting technicians and the man playing the part of Ellie's birth father. They had taken a mutual antipathy to each other early on and evidently were determined to make the most of it. Ellie's father apparently thought he was more important because he was "an actor" whilst the lighting tech pointed out, not unreasonably, that Al was more likely to need him in the future than the actor in question. It took all of Al's not inconsiderable tact and patience to keep them both placated.

Al did manage to schedule in a flying visit with Gemma—no time for sex, just a drink in the pub and a catch up, when she was on a two-day break from touring—but apart from that, he lived only for the film in a chaotic two-and-a-half weeks of hectic activity. There would be plenty to do later, but this was the really manic time where all the building blocks would be put in place for the final cut. Sometimes Al wondered why he did it, but he knew really he couldn't live without it. And by the time of the party at the end of filming on Saturday night, he knew they'd put together the ingredients for something very special.

Before he got on with anything more to do with the film, however, Al was determined to have the rest of the weekend off (including Monday, which definitely counted as weekend in Al's book). He felt like he was emerging from some sort of major illness. Possibly, he thought ruefully, that wasn't so far from the truth: he did get undeniably obsessed when he was filming. He tried to remember the last time he'd had a conversation which wasn't about *Transparent,* or messed around on the Internet on anything other than film-making websites...or even had sex. Fuck, he hadn't even wanked for the past fortnight and more.

"So, are you back in the land of the living?" Laurie asked him the morning after the film party. "If that's not a tactless question the night after a party, that is." He smiled. "I'm amazed you're here, actually—thought you'd have gone home with someone."

"Huh?" said Al, vaguely. "Oh." He cottoned on. "Never sleep with people you're working with, Laurie. Very bad plan. Especially when you're supposed to be in charge."

"Good grief, the boy does have ethics," Laurie said, mildly mocking.

Al winced a little; the comment hurt. "Just common sense," he said.

"Well." Laurie tipped Al's head up and kissed him. "I'm glad you're done for the moment. James and I have missed you. I'd suggest going out, but I reckon you've probably done more than enough of that of late. How about a quiet night in instead?"

The hurt subsided a bit because Laurie was right. There was pretty much nothing Al wanted more than a quiet night in with his housemates. It was perceptive of Laurie to have guessed that, given that Al was usually far more known for his partying. Although of late, of course—even before the filming—that had not been quite so true.

"I'd love that."

Laurie had not moved away, and he slid his arms around Al, kissing him again. "Good. We've missed our Al. And..." He hesitated. "I'm sorry about the dig about ethics. It was unfair."

Al shrugged. "Understandable."

"No," Laurie said firmly. "Unfair. So kiss me and tell me I'm forgiven?"

Which Al was definitely happy to do.

The evening went well. James cooked celebratory steak, and afterwards the three of them had celebratory sex. Al tried to think of the last time he'd been celibate so long and had to give up in the end. The filming time for his previous film, *Welding the Night Away,* had been only ten days; he suspected that meant that he'd been in his teens the last time he'd gone eighteen days without sex. Not quite like being a virgin again, he thought, amused, but probably as close as he was ever going to get. And it was good to break that run with James and Laurie, the best and most loved of his lovers.

CHAPTER FIFTEEN

Nonetheless, as the week progressed, Al knew he was suffering from post-filming burn out. It happened every time, but annoyingly, knowing what it was didn't make it any easier to deal with. Particularly because now that filming was over, he knew he had to go back to thinking about the housing situation. He'd found a couple of places and visited them. One would do fine—it was a bedsit with a large sitting/bedroom and small kitchen and bathroom in an elegant old house. It wasn't even in a particularly dodgy bit of town, which was a bonus. Al was ashamed about it but honest enough to admit, at least to himself, that he was terrified of walking alone in certain parts of the city after what had happened earlier in the year. But the place also looked horrendously lonely compared to his current situation, and Al loathed the thought of living there. If someone had told him, even a year ago, that he would hate the thought of living alone—with his own space, his own room to do what the hell he liked, to bring home who the hell he liked—he would have looked at them with utter disbelief. Not that he couldn't bring people home where he was—or do what he wanted. That was the thing; living with Laurie and James had added things to his life without taking away anything...or nothing that mattered.

Which didn't explain why he was being so bad-tempered with both his lovers. After the lovely Sunday they'd spent together, he'd turned into some sort of monster, unable to respond to anything either of them said without making some sarcastic or irritable remark. To be truthful, he was so on edge that he felt like snapping at everyone all of the time. Fen at the wine shop had only had him in for a couple of shifts post-film, but she had already commented that he seemed to have had a personality transplant. Al had apologised and tried to keep himself in order. Well as the film work was going, it was not something which he could reliably live off—especially since living alone, even in a small flat, would be more expensive than sharing.

Unfortunately for Laurie and James, and in particular James, who as Al's best friend had been on the receiving end of most of Al's barbed comments, they had not been able to rein him in in the same fashion as his boss. Even-tempered Laurie had shrugged it off and given up trying to help Al with things, waiting for him to calm down. James, however, had continued to talk to Al, trying to be supportive and presumably hoping that he would return to normal at some point. And Al was doing the best he could, but unfortunately, it wasn't a great best at the moment. Saturday night's argument started over something as petty as food.

"Do you want dinner?" James asked.

"No, I want to bloody starve," Al snapped back.

James gave him a look and then forced a laugh. "Okay, stupid question. You always want food. Any preferences?"

"Yes, for you to stop nagging." Why did James always have to make a performance out of everything? Did he really have to give Al the third degree before cooking a meal for goodness sake, Al wondered irritably.

"It doesn't sound as if Al is particularly hungry," Laurie put in calmly. "Why don't you just cook for us, James?"

"Oh, for fuck's sake," Al said impatiently. It wasn't that he didn't want to eat; he just didn't want to have a ten-hour discussion about it in advance. "I didn't mean that. I just... Never mind." He tried to dampen down his anger, but unfortunately, James wasn't finished yet.

"What do you want, then?" his friend asked.

Al exploded. "I don't bloody care, all right? Bloody hell, you're like an old woman, James. Christ, can't you do anything without a detailed list of instructions and someone to hold your hand? You're about as interesting as drying paint and about as fast moving sometimes, too. Has anyone told you that you ought to try getting a life? No wonder you usually stay in—it's not that you don't want to go out—it's that no one wants to go out with *you*."

"Al," said Laurie warningly, glancing around from his position at the desk.

Al was silent suddenly, realising that he'd gone too far. For no good reason, either. He sighed. "Fuck. Sorry. I'm being an arse."

"Yes," said James, shortly. "You are."

James was rarely that uncompromising. Al had clearly hurt him badly. He felt worse than ever. "I'm sorry. I just don't seem to be able to stop myself at the moment. I just—I've said something before I've had time to think about it. It's like I don't have any control over it."

James wouldn't look at him. Laurie stood up, saving his work. "Maybe we should help you with that," he said, his voice a little bit grim.

"What?"

Laurie looked him in the eye. "Do you want some help getting control?" he asked, and Al suddenly realised what Laurie meant.

"Yes. Please," he said. God, the thought of giving it up, of dumping all this helplessness and anger and aloneness on someone else and letting them take charge for a while... Al knew it wouldn't solve the problem, not altogether. It couldn't be solved—he was in love with two men who weren't in love with him, and there was nothing anyone could do about that. But just to have a break, to get away from his own mind for a while? He wanted that more than he could say.

"Hmph," James snorted.

"James isn't very pleased with you," Laurie commented. "Hardly surprising. So—" Laurie turned away and walked over towards the sofa, standing behind it and putting his hands on James's shoulders. "—strip and then get on your knees. And fold your clothes up neatly."

Al nodded. He wasn't quite under far enough to respond as he knew he should. James wasn't the only one who was fed up, though Al's temper was beginning to wane. He knew he'd been in the wrong, but he wasn't able to acknowledge it yet. Still, he began to remove his clothes, folding his jeans and T-shirt and placing them in a tidy pile on the floor, adding his socks and pants and then sinking to his knees, head bent and gazing at the floor, hands behind his back.

"The first thing you need to do is to make it up to James," Laurie told him coldly. "Come here and kiss his feet."

Laurie's voice washed over Al, and the first feeling of being controlled slid into the corners of his mind. Al *had* been a tosser to James, too, when James had in fact only been trying to be nice. The guilt nagged at him. Slowly, he crawled across to where James sat on the sofa, his expression still bleak. Laurie was massaging James's shoulders, soothing him, trying to calm him down after Al had riled him. It was Al's fault—James had done nothing wrong. Al could hardly blame him for not being in love, after all, however much Al wished it were so. He leaned down, removing one of James's socks and pressing a kiss to the top of his foot where James's ankle met it. Sliding down so that he was lying prostrate at James's feet, he followed it up by running a line of kisses down the high ridge to James's toes, trying to press his remorse into James's skin with each one. He nuzzled the toes, tentatively licking and sucking at them, and was rewarded by a little sigh from his lover and a slight relaxation of the tense muscles that Al had noticed, though James still would not acknowledge him.

"I'm sorry, James," he murmured, turning his attention to the other foot and doing likewise.

James's breathing was slowing, and Al could feel that his whole posture had changed from one of furious anger to something a little softer.

"You're a bastard," James said nevertheless, still cross.

"Yes, James," Al agreed humbly, continuing his ministrations, a willing supplicant begging forgiveness. Al was feeling better, too, relieved of his burden for a while, with nothing to do but what he was told. It was so freeing, giving everything up to someone else. James—god, Al would do anything for James. Though he'd had a fine way of showing it latterly, he thought guiltily. He lavished affection on James's feet, hoping that his best friend would be able to feel the extent of his regret.

"Oh, get up," James said at last, most of the rancour fading from his tone.

Al pushed himself back to his knees, still looking down. He could feel Laurie's and James's gazes on him, and he tried to look as apologetic as he was beginning to feel.

"You still need punishing," Laurie said inflexibly.

Al glanced up, a little nervously. Laurie would have forgiven insults against himself much more easily than ones aimed at James. Al was not sure how fierce his Dom's punishment might be in the circumstances. "Yes, Sir."

"Across James's lap," Laurie ordered.

Al's heart gave a little extra thump of relief. Punishment, perhaps, but it seemed he was not so unforgiven as he'd feared he might be. Laurie knew perfectly well that Al could take a great deal of pleasure out of being spanked. James had never been the one to spank him before, but Al wasn't afraid of that. James could no more hurt Al seriously than Laurie could; it wasn't in them. Obediently, Al levered himself up from the floor and draped himself over James's knees, waiting with trembling breath.

"I'm not," James informed him, giving him a sharp smack which made Al let out an involuntary squeal, "very happy with you." Smack.

"I know," Al acknowledged. He could feel the heat of James's first smacks working through his arse, painful and pleasurable together. The nerve endings fizzed, sending shockwaves out that seemed to linger in the air above his skin. "I'm sorry." Two more smacks. Al jerked, and his cock rubbed against James's legs, which added another depth of feeling. Al gasped, as the next slap caught him right between the legs, just short of his bollocks. It was followed by a sixth, further up. "Please, Jamie," he begged, rubbing up against him some more, this time with more intent.

"'James'," James corrected coldly. "I don't particularly feel like being 'Jamie' to you at the moment."

Al felt an unexpected, prickly, choking feeling in his throat. James had never said anything like that to him before. He knew he was supposed to be learning his place, but it was surprising how much that comment had hurt. Much, much worse than the spanking. James was rarely angry—not like this, and never with Al. But the worst thing was knowing he deserved it.

"James," he said quickly. "James. Please. I'm sorry. I really am." James ignored him, continuing to administer the spanks. It felt good—even as it hurt—except that Al's penitence was tearing at him. He kept silent, except for occasional yelps as harder slaps caught him on increasingly tender skin. "Please, James," he begged again at last, "I'm sorry. Please."

"I'm not"—smack—"your personal"—smack—"punching bag," James said.

"I know. Please." Between the words and the sensation, Al was shifting unbearably on James's lap. He was so fucking hard, and his arse was so hot and painful, and he wanted...he wanted all sorts of things, but mostly for James to forgive him. "I'm sorry. I'm sorry."

"What?" The spanking continued, painful and arousing simultaneously. James was in no hurry to absolve Al, it seemed.

Al found that he was choking back a sob, hating this unforgiving version of his friend and lover, hating the fact that he was responsible for it. Willing to submit to anything if only James would pardon him. "I'm sorry," he cried, his voice high and pleading. "I'm sorry."

James gave him one hard spank, making Al wince, and then unexpectedly his hand stopped smacking, resting lightly on Al's abused arse. "Okay," he said, relenting a bit. "You've got a bloody sharp tongue, though."

"I'm sorry," Al said again, his head buried on the arm of the sofa, feeling hot tears slide down his face. He wasn't sure whether pain or remorse had brought them to his eyes. "Please. I'm sorry."

He felt the moment when James relented fully, reaching out and ruffling his hair with the other hand. He stilled under James's touch, until his best friend said quietly, "Shh. You've said it enough now. I've heard you. I've heard. It's okay."

"And now," Laurie commented from above them, his voice also softer now that James had expressed his forgiveness, "perhaps it's time we reminded Al of where he does belong; do you think James?"

"That sounds like a good idea," James said.

"Al?"

"Yes, Sir," Al said obediently, docile and willing to do whatever they wanted. He could have lain here forever, under James's now-gentle hands, but if something was required of him, then of course he would obey. Anything. *Anything.*

Laurie leaned further over the back of the sofa and kissed James firmly on the mouth. Al could feel James turning in his seat to open his mouth under Laurie's, deepening and lengthening the kiss.

"Do you remember the first time we fucked Al?" Laurie asked James, after a long pause.

"Mm-hmm." Al could hear the smile in James's voice.

"Apparently he needs to be reminded that he belongs to us. It strikes me that it would be a good way of reminding him."

Al caught his breath. Their first time together, James and Laurie had both penetrated him at once. It had been amazing. They'd done it a couple of times since, but it was rare—the other two were concerned about hurting him, despite Al's protestations. They were of larger build than he was, and Laurie at least, was considerably more than averagely endowed. Nonetheless, Al loved the feeling of both of them inside him, filling him so full he could think of nothing else.

"Please," he whispered, longingly.

James gave him another smack, albeit a gentle one. "Not your choice, Al."

"No, James," Al agreed quietly, ashamed.

"Do you want to be ordered to be silent again?" Laurie demanded.

"No, Sir. Please, no." Al knew he would not be able to keep to it, not with both of them fucking him. He didn't think he could bear to let them down again today. "I'm sorry. I'll try not to speak."

"Good boy." James hitched him over and kissed him lightly on the lips. "You can be so good, Al," he said softly.

Al felt himself warming to the praise. He looked at James in adoring silence, grateful for this new sign of forgiveness. Laurie leaned down and kissed Al in turn, before coming round to join the other two on the sofa.

"Now, Al," Laurie said, leaning over him, "You need to undress James and me first, don't you? So, on the floor with you, please."

"Yes, Sir." Al scrambled to the floor, wincing slightly as his freshly spanked arse came into contact with the carpet unexpectedly. "James?" he asked, seeking permission as his hands came up towards James's belt, scared of accidentally misbehaving.

"Go on, then," James said. He put his hands over Al's for a second, warm and reassuring, understanding how much Al needed that when he was under like this. "It's okay. You're forgiven," he told him.

Al bent his head a little. "Thank you."

His fingers worked carefully on unfastening James's belt and then opening his trousers. James shifted to allow him to pull them down with his pants, and Al's fingers lingered for as long as he dared on James's erection as he went past. James gave a soft laugh but made no complaint, and Al's eyes fluttered shut for a second. God, he loved touching James, and the relief he was feeling that James was no longer angry was ineffable. He wanted to press kisses to the insides of James's thighs, to sit here between his lover's legs and touch every inch of his skin. To worship him, almost. But Laurie was waiting, and while Al loved James, he loved Laurie as much. He was drawn to James because of the desperate wish to make up to him for taking his bad temper out on him earlier, but Laurie had helped him out of that position and he was more grateful to Laurie for that than he could say.

He moved over to Laurie, and began to perform the same task on him, undressing him with careful gestures until both of his lovers were only wearing their tops. Laurie had reached a hand over to James and curled it around his boyfriend's erection, sliding it to and fro with a familiar gesture. James, with a little grunt of pleasure, leaned his head back against the sofa; Al watched James's body react to Laurie's ministrations as he dragged Laurie's trousers off and folded them carefully with his own. James was so bloody gorgeous.

"Now," Laurie said, Al still kneeling between his legs, "you're going to suck my cock. Make it all wet, Al, because you're going to fuck yourself on it in a minute."

Al bit back a little protest, raising scared eyes to Laurie for a second. It was not the idea of fucking himself on Laurie that concerned him, but Laurie surely didn't mean that Al was supposed to take both Laurie *and* James inside him with just a bit of saliva to slick the way? Al was hardly virginal, but he wasn't sure he could cope with that. He knew he was in disgrace, and he would go through with it if Laurie demanded it of him, but the thought was terrifying.

Laurie pressed one finger to his face. "Lube as well," he said, reading Al's thoughts accurately. "We're not going to kill you, Al."

Al, whose heart had started beating uncomfortably hard, relaxed a little and leaned forward to take Laurie's cock into his mouth. It was large, and it had taken Al some practice to be able to get his jaw round much more than half of it, but at the same time, he loved the feeling of a cock in his mouth, and in many ways Laurie's size made it more rewarding still. The first moment Al had seen it, he'd wanted to suck it. Plus, it was Laurie's, and Al would take any part of Laurie or James any way he could get. Especially right now. His hand on the base of Laurie's shaft, Al closed his eyes and gave in to the sensation. He rocked back and forth, running his tongue around the ridges as his hand worked the lower part of Laurie's cock.

"Lean forward," Laurie murmured after a bit. "Let James prep you a bit."

Al obediently changed position so that his arse was exposed, sliding his legs further apart. He felt James's hand against his skin and took a pained, gasping breath around Laurie's cock; his arse was undeniably sore from James's firmly delivered spanking.

"God, your skin's on fire," James said quietly, sliding his hand between Al's legs and touching the pucker of his hole with slippery fingers. Al moaned, but said nothing; the noise he made sent shivers through Laurie. "He looks gorgeous, though," James said to Laurie above his head, pushing inside Al with first one, and then two fingers. "Like he's begging to be fucked."

"He probably is."

Al thought, not for the first time, how sensual Laurie's deep voice was. The words felt like touches against his skin. He moaned again, shifting against James's fingers, and James laughed.

"I think you're right."

He pistoned his fingers in and out of Al, stretching him. Al felt his eyes flutter closed at the sensation, combined with the taste and feeling of Laurie in his mouth. His jaw was beginning to ache at the distension of his mouth, but at the same time he wanted to continue doing this forever. James changed the angle of his touch, pressing against Al's prostate, and Al felt as if he were drowning in pleasure.

"He likes that," he heard Laurie comment as if from far away.

"I'd noticed." James's tone was amused. He scissored his fingers wider, adding a third, a fourth, before saying, "I think he could take you easily enough now."

"Okay." Laurie pushed Al away from his cock with appropriate carefulness. "Now, Al, I'm going to lie on the sofa here, and you're going to slide down onto me. But" —his voice was very serious, and Al looked up to meet stern blue eyes— "you need to learn control, don't you? You've been out of control this evening. So James and I are going to fuck you, but you're not going to come. You're not even going to touch yourself, is that understood? You're going to let us do what we want with you, and you'll take it all like a good boy."

Al shivered slightly. He wasn't sure he could do it. But Laurie's orders must be obeyed at all costs tonight, of all times.

"Yes, Sir," he whispered.

"You're just going to be ours," Laurie said, sliding down onto the sofa and pulling Al on top of him. "Do what we want, how we want. Your needs aren't important. You'll concentrate just on us, making it good for us." He paused. "Make it good for us, Al," he said, running his hands over Al's body.

"Yes, Sir."

Al positioned himself over Laurie, and with Laurie's help, guided himself onto his lover. There was a moment of resistance, and then he gave a sigh of relief as Laurie began to bury himself inside him. It felt good—too good. The desire to touch himself was so damn strong. Instead, he watched Laurie's face, trying to concentrate on doing what Laurie wanted—what would make Laurie feel best. A tremor went through him, nonetheless; Laurie's eyes were dark pupilled and possessive and filled with desire, and oh, Al loved Laurie fucking him.

"Deeper. Further," Laurie encouraged, hands moving to Al's sides to hold him.

He was not supposed to be speaking. Al bit back the 'oh god' on the tip of his tongue, letting out a wordless cry instead. Too good. Fuck. His hand was clenched so hard against the arm of the sofa that his knuckles were white with the strain. He couldn't take this. He couldn't do this without touching himself—not with James not even inside him yet. Laurie took a deep breath, and Al knew his lover was resisting the urge to fuck up into him. So much control over himself as well as over Al. Al needed to show he could do well for Laurie and James, prove his repentance for acting like a jerk. He kept his gaze locked on Laurie's as James slid a finger inside him next to Laurie's cock. It slipped in so easily despite Laurie's girth. Al pushed back against it, pushing Laurie's cock and James's finger in as deeply as possible.

"Such a little slut, aren't you?" Laurie said fondly.

Al moaned, rocking back and forth and trying to ignore his painfully aching cock. If he pushed back hard enough against James, the palm of James's hand struck his abused arse, the pain a slight distraction from his need. James pushed another finger in beside him. This time, the size noticed, Al hissed at the sensation. So full. So very full. Good. Glorious. Impossible to cope with. He needed to touch himself so badly. His breath caught in his chest.

"Relax," said James, behind him.

"I can't," Al choked out. He took a gasping breath, looking pleadingly at Laurie. "Please—please, Sir, please could you—hold down my hands," he begged desperately. He had to touch himself. He couldn't bear it. But he couldn't let Laurie down, disobey. Laurie wanted him to stay in control, but it was so difficult when his cock was this fucking hard. "Please." He was trembling with the effort needed to prevent himself thrusting a hand between his legs right now.

"Oh, Al," Laurie said chidingly. "You've managed not to touch yourself before."

"But Jamie—J-James," Al corrected himself, with a quick hitch in his speech, "helped last time. And the time before, he had his mouth on my cock. Please, Sir, please—I can't—"

"Okay," Laurie soothed, clasping strong fingers around Al's wrists and holding them down by his sides.

James kissed Al's back, mouthing his way down it. "Jamie is okay," he reassured Al. "Forgiven, remember?"

"Please, Jamie, I need you," Al whined, as James pressed a third finger into him, stretching him so damn open. He wanted James's cock so much. Wanted to make it good for James.

"Control," Laurie said sharply.

Al whimpered, squeezing his eyes shut and biting down into his lip to keep himself from begging some more. His hands still twitched with the longing to get at his cock, but Laurie's grip was strong and firm and even when Al went to lift his arm, unable to bear not to, he was unable to move it. He shoved back against James's fingers again, and James ran his other hand down his back.

"So impatient," James scolded.

Al was taking deep, sobbing breaths, unable to concentrate on anything but his need to be filled, his desire to touch himself. He was barely aware of his own name, who he was—he was nothing but this aching, hypersensitive body. And James switched fingers for cock, pressing in slowly and sliding his way in, his cock and Laurie's filling Al so damn full that Al was actually crying with the need, with his struggle not to speak and not to touch, when he felt like he was going crazy for it. He was going to come without even touching, and he mustn't—he mustn't. He fought against Laurie's grip on his wrists, not because he wanted to get free but to distract himself from his desperation through the discomfort of tugging against a steel-trap hold, grateful for Laurie's strength and the knowledge that he couldn't get free, no matter how much he struggled. Grateful too for the knowledge that Laurie wouldn't let go, trusting him to safeword if needed.

James began rutting inside him, Laurie staying still, concentrating on holding Al. It felt, it felt—god—so good, so full. Al could feel the tears rolling down his face and hoped it was as good for his lovers as it was for him. James's hoarse breathing was mixed with occasional curse words, his fingers digging into Al's skin. Laurie's fingers were tight on Al's wrists; he would be bruised in the morning, he knew. A beautiful thought. He tried to stay still, let his lovers do what they wanted with him, be nothing but the source of their pleasure. Tried to think about anything, anything at all but his need to come, his utter desperation. Just as he thought he could not stand it another moment, Laurie bucked underneath him just once.

"Jamie. Al," Laurie groaned, and then he was spasming inside Al, filling Al with his come.

Al was keening, an impossible noise coming from his throat, because Laurie had said his name, *said his fucking name*, and Al had no idea how he wasn't coming, except that it was the only thing he could do for Laurie in return.

James said, "Oh fuck, oh fuck."

And then both Al's lovers were coming inside him, and Al could do nothing but take it, his body on fire, the tears coursing down his face as he cried out on that one desperate note.

Laurie's breathing was shaky, and he was blinking fast. James had his head on Al's shoulder, his arms tightly around him. Then, as James slid out of his arse, Laurie let go of Al's wrists.

"Touch yourself, Al," he said, his voice husky and needy. "Bring yourself off for me and James, baby."

James lifted his head a little, and Al knew he was watching, just as Laurie also had hot, eager eyes on him. It took so little, so damn little, the slightest touch of his fingers to his cock, the feeling of the hot come running out of his arse as he moved. One stroke, two, and Al was bursting with it, riding waves that took him over and over again until he could barely see, hear, think. All was sensation, and the world was spinning on its axis and could have come apart entirely right now, and Al wouldn't have cared. And he was gathered up in two pairs of strong arms, held closely against hot, sticky bodies, and the tears which had run down his face as he struggled to obey Laurie's commands were still falling; Al thought he had perhaps never cried so much in his life.

"Shh, shh." He could hear Laurie whispering in his ear; there was a hand stroking his head, and another his back whilst two more arms were tangled around him. He was safe, owned, surrounded. Whilst he was still trying to bring himself back from the brink, he was accosted by an unexpected question from James.

"Why do you want to move out?"

"James," Laurie said reproachfully, "is this the moment?"

But Al was still in the sub mindset. Not answering a direct question was unthinkable. "Because I broke my rule," he whispered, glancing down. "I fell in love." He couldn't look at James or Laurie.

Laurie shrugged himself, and perforce Al, up to sitting. James slid up so that he was next to Laurie with Al across their laps. Laurie was tense; Al could feel it, but James... James's posture looked negative, almost defeated.

"Gemma?" James asked bleakly.

Laurie put his hand on James's. "James, I don't think he means Gemma." He put his hand to Al's cheek and turned him to face them. "Do you?" Al shook his head. "You, James," Laurie said quietly.

Al made a little noise of objection.

"Laurie?" James asked.

"Both," Al muttered, looking away. "Love both of you. Need you."

"You need us?" James said, a breathless sort of hush in his tone.

Al nodded, hiding his face against James. Feeling too exposed. This wasn't right; this wasn't what he did. James's arms went round him. Jamie would always hold him when he needed it, just as he'd done when he'd woken Al from the nightmare. No demands; James was always there for him. Where the hell had *that* thought just come from?

"Why do you want to leave?" James asked again, his breath warm against Al's hair.

"Scared." The vulnerability of subspace let Al say things he could never have said in other circumstances. Things he hadn't even realised were true. "Don't belong."

Laurie's arms joined James's round Al. "Yes, you do."

Why was there something so reassuring about Laurie's deep voice, about the strength of his arms? Something so familiar and reliable about James's hold?

"I was only here because you felt sorry for me. Not supposed to be staying forever. You're a couple. I—"

"You belong with us," Laurie said, as calmly as if it wasn't even something which needed discussion.

"We told you we loved you when we asked you to stay," James added. He sounded as if Al had deliberately hurt him somehow. "We wanted you. We want you."

"Because you're my friends."

"No." The correction came from both Laurie and James.

"Not just that," James added.

"Oh." Al tried to process this. Failed. They were being kind now, but only because they knew how he felt, not because they meant anything by it. He should never have told them. It was only that idiot submissive part of his brain which had let it out.

"We realised we couldn't do without you," Laurie said. "James told you he wanted you to live with us. I only said 'for a bit' when you wouldn't accept we wanted you forever. I didn't want to lose you entirely by pushing too hard."

"That's not true."

No one had wanted Al forever. Not even his parents. Especially not them. Why would anyone else? Why would anyone like James and Laurie want him—love him—particularly when they had each other?

If you had asked most people—even Al himself—they would have said Al Hitchins had a pretty good opinion of himself. Too good, many would say. But there had always been this gap, this void inside. The knowledge that he was more or less unlovable. It had been there since he was a child, hearing the regret and exasperation in his parents' voices when they spoke of him, knowing they wished they'd never had a son. He'd tucked the hurt away, learned to live with it until it was so much a part of him that he never even thought to consider it any more. It just *was*. Al was not the sort of person who could be loved, and that was fine—one of those things about him, like the fact he was bisexual, or he had a fascination with films. Part of him. An immutable fact. Hearing it challenged was in some strange way more painful than living with the knowledge of its existence. And a million times more terrifying. He couldn't believe. He daren't believe.

Hope *hurt*.

"Actually," James said, "it is."

Al shook his head dumbly.

"You really don't believe that, do you?" Laurie asked gently.

"Like I haven't needed and relied on him for the last god knows how long," James said.

"Not since you've had Laurie."

"Oh yes," James said, "even then. Still now." He gave Al a smile. "Didn't want to fall in love with you, mind. That seemed a bit much, especially when you'd told me that you'd fear for your sanity if you ever wanted a relationship with me."

Al blushed. He remembered saying more or less those very words, many years ago, though it hadn't been as tactless as James made it sound; at the time, he'd been reassuring James rather than insulting him. James had been in love with an inaccessible Laurie and in need of sex without strings, which was something Al had been quite willing to provide. He hadn't anticipated having his words quoted back to him some five or six years later—certainly not in the present circumstances—

whatever they might be. Al still wasn't sure. It was hard to doubt James's sincerity, but—

"But Laurie—" Al objected.

"Suggested you move in with us in the first place," James said. "Even admitted he was 'a bit' in love with you." James's words were spoken so bluntly, they were clearly true. Especially given the colour rising on Laurie's face.

"I'm not going to apologise," Laurie said, ignoring his own embarrassment rather superbly, Al thought. "Or pretend James is lying. Though I'd like to point out that James didn't deny feeling the same way about you, either. I knew when I said I wanted you here it wouldn't matter to you whether you lived with us or not. But it mattered to me. And it mattered to Jamie. You might not give a toss what happened to you, but we did." His voice roughened. "God, Al, don't you know James would die for you? And I found out a few months ago that I'd fucking kill for you. The people who raped you? I'd kill them so damn easily."

Al realised he had stopped breathing. There was nothing he could say. No way he could deny what his friends—his lovers—his *loves* were saying. The men he loved, loved him back.

"You don't..." he began.

"Oh, shut up," said his best friend, lover—and love, smiling at him and placing a long kiss on his lips.

Al looked up to see Laurie gazing at them both with the tenderness he associated with Laurie's gaze at James alone. It was hard to believe that part of that was for him. But he still had other things to speak about—important ones. They might yet change their minds. Al might be in love, but he was still Al. He was who he was, and he wouldn't go into any relationship that was based on a lie.

"I won't be faithful to you, you know," he said soberly. Slowly, he was beginning to return to his normal self...if he even knew what that was any more after the world had spun so greatly in such a short space of time.

Laurie and James regarded him with love in their eyes.

"Yes you will," James said.

"You'll sleep with plenty of other people," Laurie added, "but that's a different matter."

"Oh." Al had not thought about it that way before—that chastity and fidelity were not one and the same. He looked back at them, brain entirely clear now of the fog of subspace. He was grateful to the fog, though; without it, he could never have said what he had. "Yes, I suppose it is."

"You've already been faithful to me for fifteen years," James pointed out.

The back-to-normal version of Al squirmed at this. "Don't say that. It sounds wrong!"

James grinned. "True, though, and you know it. In every way that matters."

It was. And Al knew also that his lovers were right when they said he would be faithful. He was intensely, impossibly loyal at heart. There were no circumstances in which he would not love James, he knew; life had already proved that. And he was certain in his heart it would be no different with Laurie—indeed, that it had not been for some time. But that they should love him back...

"And you..." Al looked from one of them to the other, still struggling to believe.

"We love you," said James.

"We want you. And, for the record, we want you just as you are. Not some strange, so-called 'better' version. This Al, the one who sleeps around and can't cook, and stays up half the night doing manic things when he's in the middle of a film." Laurie smiled. "A bit less yelling at James might be good, but—"

"Sorry," Al said apologetically to his best friend. "It was...the moving thing was doing my head in."

"Looks like Laurie's found a way of keeping you in order, anyway," James retorted.

Al ducked his head in embarrassment. The idea of subspace was very weird when you weren't in it. Granted, he had much to be grateful to it for, but still.

"Unkind, Jamie," Laurie said chidingly.

James gave the little huff of amusement that was so specifically him. "But I can say accurately, 'Al knows I love him really' now, though, can't I?"

Laurie and Al both laughed at this. "Yes," admitted Laurie. "I suppose you can." He stared firmly at Al. "So, no more of this moving out business, yeah?" he asked.

"Not unless you throw me out," Al assured him.

"And...well..." Laurie looked awkward.

"What?"

"Well, obviously you'll still need your own room for entertainment purposes, but maybe" —Laurie sounded tentative, which seemed very un-Laurie-like— "when you're not needing it... Look, our bed's big enough for three, as you know." Al had indeed slept in it on several occasions in the past. "James doesn't snore—much," Laurie added. James—who did not snore at all, as Al knew, having shared a room with him regularly over the past fifteen years—poked his boyfriend at this. "Nor do I. And it'll save Jamie having to get up if you have a nightmare," Laurie finished persuasively.

"Unkind, Laurie," mocked James.

"Pasta," said Al, unexpectedly. He grinned as the other two stared at him. "What? James asked me, a while back, what I wanted for tea. I fancy pasta. With something tomato-y, preferably. And then a large bed with two largish men, both of whom I happen to be desperately in love with. Any complaints?"

And from James's and Laurie's reactions, it seemed there were none.

About the Author

P.A. Friday fails dismally to write one sort of thing and, when not writing erotica and erotic romance of all sexualities, may be found writing articles on the Regency period, pagan poetry, or science fiction. She loves wine and red peppers, and loathes coffee and mushrooms.

Email: penfriday@gmail.com
Website: http://www.penelopefriday.com
Twitter: @penelopefriday
Facebook: http://www.facebook.com/penelopefriday

Also by P.A. Friday

All About the Boy

NINESTAR PRESS, LLC

www.ninestarpress.com

www.ingramcontent.com/pod-product-compliance
Lightning Source LLC
Chambersburg PA
CBHW022121170626
46808CB00002B/799